HARLEQUIN®
Presents

At Harlequin Presents we are always interested in what you, the readers, think about the series. So if you have any thoughts you'd like to share, please join in the discussion of your favorite books at www.iheartpresents.com—created by and for fans of Harlequin Presents!

On the site, find blog entries written by authors and fans, the inside scoop from editors and links to authors and books. Enjoy and share with others the unique world of Presents— we'd love to hear from you!

D0558682

Harlequin Presents®

They're the men who have everything—
except brides...

Wealth, power, charm—
what else could a heart-stoppingly handsome
tycoon need? In the GREEK TYCOONS
miniseries, you have already been introduced to
some gorgeous Greek multimillionaires who are
in need of wives.

Now it's the turn of popular Harlequin Presents
author Kate Hewitt, with her sensual romance
The Greek Tycoon's Convenient Bride

This tycoon has met his match, and he's decided
he *has* to have her...*whatever* that takes!

DON

Kate Hewitt

THE GREEK TYCOON'S CONVENIENT BRIDE

Newport Public Library
316 North Fourth Street
Newport, PA 17074

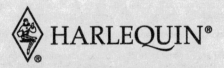

HARLEQUIN®

TORONTO • NEW YORK • LONDON
AMSTERDAM • PARIS • SYDNEY • HAMBURG
STOCKHOLM • ATHENS • TOKYO • MILAN • MADRID
PRAGUE • WARSAW • BUDAPEST • AUCKLAND

If you purchased this book without a cover you should be aware
that this book is stolen property. It was reported as "unsold and
destroyed" to the publisher, and neither the author nor the
publisher has received any payment for this "stripped book."

ISBN-13: 978-0-373-12722-1
ISBN-10:   0-373-12722-7

THE GREEK TYCOON'S CONVENIENT BRIDE

First North American Publication 2008.

Copyright © 2007 by Kate Hewitt.

All rights reserved. Except for use in any review, the reproduction or
utilization of this work in whole or in part in any form by any electronic,
mechanical or other means, now known or hereafter invented, including
xerography, photocopying and recording, or in any information storage
or retrieval system, is forbidden without the written permission of the
publisher, Harlequin Enterprises Limited, 225 Duncan Mill Road,
Don Mills, Ontario, Canada M3B 3K9.

This is a work of fiction. Names, characters, places and incidents are
either the product of the author's imagination or are used fictitiously,
and any resemblance to actual persons, living or dead, business
establishments, events or locales is entirely coincidental.

This edition published by arrangement with Harlequin Books S.A.

® and TM are trademarks of the publisher. Trademarks indicated with
® are registered in the United States Patent and Trademark Office, the
Canadian Trade Marks Office and in other countries.

www.eHarlequin.com

Printed in U.S.A.

All about the author...
Kate Hewitt

KATE HEWITT discovered her first Harlequin romance on a trip to England when she was thirteen, and she's continued to read them ever since. She wrote her first story at the age of five, simply because her older brother had written one and she thought she could do it, too. That story was one sentence long—fortunately, they've become a bit more detailed as she's grown older.

She studied drama in college and shortly after graduation moved to New York City to pursue a career in theater. This was derailed by something far better—meeting the man of her dreams, who happened also to be her older brother's childhood friend. Ten days after their wedding they moved to England, where Kate worked a variety of different jobs—drama teacher, editorial assistant, youth worker, secretary and finally mother.

When her oldest daughter was a year old, Kate sold her first short story to a British magazine. Since then she has sold many stories and serials, but writing romance remains her first love—of course!

Besides writing, she enjoys reading, traveling and learning to knit—it's an ongoing process and she's made a lot of scarves. After living in England for six years, she now resides in Connecticut with her husband, her three young children and, perhaps someday, a dog.

Kate loves to hear from readers, You can contact her through her Web site, www.kate-hewitt.com.

PROLOGUE

HE WATCHED her from the shadows.

Lukas Petrakides stood behind the camouflaging fronds of a palm tree, his eyes tracking the young woman as she slipped from her hotel room onto the silky sand of the beach.

Dark, wild curls blew around her face and her slender arms crept around herself in a hug that was pitiably vulnerable.

He hadn't meant to stumble upon her—or anyone—here. He'd been consumed with a restless energy, his mind full of plans for the new resort that had just opened here in the Languedoc, minutes from a sleepy village, stretching out to a pristine beach.

He'd needed to escape the confines of his own suite, his own mind, even if just for a moment.

The wind and the waves shimmering beneath a diamond sky had soothed him, and he'd slipped off his shoes, rolled up the cuffs of his trousers, and strode down the smooth, white sand.

And had found her.

He didn't know what had drawn him to her, why that slender form seemed to hold so much grace, beauty, desire.

Sorrow.

Her head was bowed, her shoulders slightly slumped. The look of someone in grief or pain.

Still he felt a blaze of feeling deep within. A need. A connection.

He took one step towards her, an impulse, an instinct, before checking himself. He knew his presence here would cause questions, complications he couldn't afford.

He had to keep his reputation above the faintest reproach. He always had. So he stood in the shadows, watched her walk towards the waves, and wondered.

She stood on the shore, the waves lapping her bare feet, and gazed out at the calm waters of the Mediterranean. She threw one worried glance over her shoulder towards the sliding glass door of her hotel room, as if someone were there, waiting, watching, as he was.

Who waited for her in there? A boyfriend? Husband?

A lover?

Whoever it was, it was none of his business.

If he were a different man—with a different life, different responsibilities—he might not check that impulse. He might walk up to her, say hello, make conversation.

Nothing sleazy or sordid; he didn't want that. Just honest conversation, a shared moment. Something real and warm and alive.

The desire for it shook him, vibrated deep in his being. He shook his head. It was never going to happen.

A bitter smile twisted his lips as he watched her. She dropped her arms, raised her face to the moon-bathed sky. The breeze off the sea moulded her cheap sundress to the slight contours of her body. Her curves were boyish at best, yet Lukas still felt a stirring of desire.

A desire he wouldn't act upon. Couldn't. As the only son of his father, the only heir to the Petrakides real estate fortune, he carried too many responsibilities to shrug them off lightly for a mere dalliance with a slip of a girl. For a moment's connection.

He would never let it be anything more.

His grey eyes hardened to pewter. He thought he heard her give a little shuddering sigh, but perhaps it was the wind. Perhaps it was his imagination.

Perhaps that sound had come from him.

She jerked her head around sharply, and he drew in a breath

as he stepped back, deeper into the shadows. Had he made a
sound—one that she'd heard?

Her gaze swept the beach, fastened on the sliding glass door
to her hotel room. She hadn't seen him, he realised; something
from inside the room—a person? A man?—had beckoned her.

Her body sagged slightly, her arms dropping to her sides, her
head bowed as she turned to head back inside.

Lukas watched her go, wondered who—what—had called
her. Why did she look so sorrowful, as if the weight of the world
rested on those slight shoulders?

He knew how that felt. He understood about crippling weight.

The sliding glass door closed with a click, and, suppressing
another wave of longing, Lukas turned to head back to his
private suite.

CHAPTER ONE

RHIANNON DAVIES checked her reflection one last time before nodding to the babysitter.

'Right...I should only be an hour or two.' She glanced uncertainly at the baby sitting on the floor, chewing on her house keys and looking at her with dark, soulful eyes. 'She might need a nap in a little while.'

The babysitter, a stout Frenchwoman with an impassive expression, nodded once before stooping to pick Annabel up in her arms.

Rhiannon watched, noticed how the older woman's arms went comfortably around Annabel's chubby middle and carried her with a confident ease she had yet to feel herself.

'I don't think she'll cry,' she ventured, and was answered with another brisk nod.

In the two weeks since Annabel had been in her care, the baby had hardly cried at all. Despite the whirl of events, the change of both home and mother, she simply regarded the world with big, blank eyes. Rhiannon suspected the poor mite was in shock.

That was why she was here, she told herself firmly, not for the first time, ignoring the pangs of guilt and longing stabbing her middle. Her heart.

She had come to France, to this exclusive resort, to Lukas Petrakides, to give Annabel some stability. To give her love.

Annabel stuck a fist in her mouth and chewed while gazing in blank curiosity at the woman who'd come so abruptly into her life.

Rhiannon.

They hadn't bonded, Rhiannon acknowledged, hadn't really tried. It was too strange, too difficult, too sad.

She'd never even held a baby before Leanne, pale-faced, wide-eyed, had thrust a sleeping Annabel into her arms. *Take her.*

Rhiannon's arms had closed around the solid little form as a matter of instinct, but her arms had been at awkward angles and she hadn't been sure how to cuddle.

Annabel had woken up with a furious screech.

'Goodbye, sweetheart.' Hesitantly Rhiannon stroked one satiny cheek. Annabel simply blinked.

It was better this way, she knew. Better they didn't get attached. Then it would be so much easier to say goodbye.

A lump formed in her throat; she forced it down. She would do what she had to do to secure Annabel's future and, more importantly, her happiness.

No matter what the cost.

She stole one last look at her reflection: dark curls, mostly tamed behind her ears, a face pale but with a sprinkling of freckles in stark relief, a smart if inexpensive skirt, and a matching sleeveless top in aquamarine. Modest, businesslike. Appropriate.

Suppressing a sigh, she slipped out of the hotel room.

The sun was bright, the air fresh and clean as she walked along the outside corridor. The newest Petra Resort, situated in this remote, exclusive corner of the Languedoc province of France, was simple, spare and elegant. Having arrived in darkness, she now took note of the bougainvillaea spilling from terracotta pots, the climbing vines, the clean colours.

It had cost her half a month's salary—far more than she could possibly afford—to book even the cheapest room at the resort on its opening weekend. If there hadn't been a last-minute cancellation she wouldn't have got in at all.

Taking a deep, cleansing breath that was meant to steady her jangling nerves, Rhiannon hoped this journey would be worth it. For Annabel.

She closed her eyes briefly. This was all so, so crazy.

Only a fortnight ago Leanne had exploded back into her life—and out again just as quickly. Leaving confusion and Annabel in her wake. And the name of Annabel's father.

Rhiannon bit her lip as fresh doubts assailed her, washed over her in a sickening wave. What if Lukas refused to talk to her? Or, worse, denied his responsibility? When she'd attempted to contact him by telephone she hadn't made it past the first hurdle.

We'll give Mr Petrakides your message.

Yeah, right. The disbelief and scorn had been obvious, shaming. They hadn't even taken her number or her name.

Then she'd read in the local newspaper that a new Petra resort was opening in France, seen that Lukas Petrakides would be there at a reception for the resort's first guests. She knew it was a chance—perhaps the only one—for Annabel to know her father. Her family.

Every child needed parents. Real ones, not strangers who took them out of duty, obligation.

She believed that with all her heart. She wanted more for Annabel. She wanted to give her a family. She didn't know where she herself would fit into that equation, if at all. The thought had first chilled her; now it merely numbed.

She understood about sacrifice. She was prepared.

Rhiannon walked down several corridors, looking for the lounge that the resort had advertised as the location for the 'Meet and Greet' reception.

Whenever a new Petra resort opened—and now there had to be half a dozen—Lukas Petrakides, the founder's son and CEO of the company, came to meet with his guests.

His fans, Rhiannon thought wryly. For since learning the name of Annabel's father, she'd researched the man and come up with some information. Although reclusive, Lukas Petrakides was adored by the Greek public and press alike—considered broodingly handsome, unfailingly polite, stunningly charismatic.

Rhiannon smiled at the thought. Surely the magazines had to be making some of that up?

They had to make something up, for Lukas Petrakides was notorious for not providing gossip for the rumour mill. Unlike other Mediterranean tycoons, he didn't appear in public with the latest model or starlet on his arm. His only escort was one of his three older sisters. Photographs were rare. He didn't party, didn't drink, didn't dance.

Didn't do much of anything, it seemed, except work.

Considering such a reputation, Rhiannon couldn't quite dismiss the faint sense of disbelief that Lukas Petrakides had, at least on one occasion, put aside his own responsibilities for a weekend of no-strings romance. Sex.

One person had cracked his armour and found if not his heart then his libido.

Leanne... And the result of that union was back in her hotel room.

Rhiannon dragged in a shuddering breath, needing the air, the courage. She hadn't been able to formulate a plan beyond the basic: book two nights' accommodation at the Petra Resort, attend the reception, find Lukas Petrakides.

And then...?

Her mind skittered frantically, in time with her rapid pulse, even as her heart provided the answer.

And then he'll want her. He'll love her, he'll take her into his home, his heart. They'll be a family, happy, loving, perfect. The End.

Rhiannon's mouth twisted in painful acknowledgement of this fairy tale. Life didn't work that way. It hadn't for her.

But surely it could for Annabel?

She knew Lukas was a man of responsibility; the tabloids held him up as a paragon. It was his shining reputation for integrity, honour, and an unfailing sense of duty that had made the decision for Rhiannon.

This was a man who could—and she prayed would—take on the mantle of fatherhood without a qualm or quiver. A man who would welcome his daughter with open arms.

She finally came to a pair of double doors, guarded by two impassive-looking security guards who asked for her room number.

One of them scanned a list. 'Name?'

'Rhiannon Davies.' Her heart pounded but at least her voice sounded calm.

The guard nodded brusquely, and Rhiannon was given entry. She slipped between the doors, taking in the diamond-spangled crowd with a sinking heart.

She didn't fit in here, and it was obvious. This was a party for the rich and famous, or at least the socially savvy. Not her. Never her.

She scanned the room, a blush rising to her cheeks as she caught the curious stares, the scornful looks. She knew her outfit was inexpensive, but it was hardly tawdry or inappropriate. Yet Rhiannon felt as if she was standing there naked by the way a few well-heeled, skimpily clad society she-devils were looking at her.

For heaven's sake, *they* were wearing fewer clothes than she was. She lifted her chin, stiffened her spine. She didn't care what anyone thought about her; all that mattered was getting to Lukas.

Telling him about Annabel.

She scanned the room again, took a few steps inside. And saw him.

Once her gaze fastened on his form, she wondered how she could have missed him for a moment. He was tall—taller than most men—dressed in an elegant grey suit, perfectly cut, moulding to his powerful shoulders and trim hips. He leaned against the bar, a drink in one hand, although Rhiannon saw it was virtually untouched.

She saw his suave smile, imagined she could hear his dry chuckle across the room, watched his graceful movements. And still the thought sprang unbidden into her mind.

He's unhappy. He's lonely.

She shook her head slightly; the idea was ridiculous. Who could be either lonely or unhappy with the crème of society jostling for his attention, for one word from those sculpted lips?

She almost laughed at herself; Lukas Petrakides was every bit as handsome as the tabloids claimed he was. She had expected to be intimidated; she hadn't expected to be affected.

Squaring her shoulders, Rhiannon waded into the expensive fray. She walked towards the bar, stopping a few feet before the man himself.

Uncertainty washed over her with the scent of expensive, cloying perfume from the women jostling her, queuing for Lukas's attention. She hadn't considered the crowds, the difficulty in approaching him. She should have.

She nibbled at her lip as she considered her options. She wanted to speak in private, but she doubted a man like Lukas Petrakides would consider a request for a private conversation from a person like her—plain, poor, socially irrelevant.

Still, there wasn't much else she could do. This was why she had come. Phone calls and letters could be ignored, dismissed. Face to face it would be more difficult for him to ignore or deny...if she was able to speak to him at all.

She was just about to take a step forward when he turned. Saw her. Looked at her almost as if he recognised her...*knew* her. And she felt a sudden penetrating flash of awareness come over her like a shiver, a shock—as if *she* knew him. Impossible. Ridiculous.

Still, the expression in his eyes dried her mouth, her words. Her thoughts. His eyes had been described in the tabloids as grey, but Rhiannon decided that they were silver, the colour of a rain-washed river. A small, tender smile quirked his mouth upwards.

He raised an eyebrow, gestured to the space next to him at the bar even as a matron droned on in French at his other side.

Rhiannon's pulse kicked into gear and a strange new sensation flooded through her—pleasant, fizzy, limb-weakening.

Desire.

All it had taken was one smile, one look from those piercing eyes, one tiny glimmer of tenderness, and she was hooked. Caught.

Was she that desperate? That obvious?

Yet she couldn't deny the connection that seemed to pulse between them across the crowded room, as present and real as if a wire stretched between them, drawing her to him.

She walked towards him, towards the heat flaring in his gaze, as if it were a place she had always meant to go. To be.

He watched, a faint smile curving those exquisite lips, lighting his eyes.

Then she stumbled, caught herself on the bar. Her slick palms curled around cool marble. She heard the low titter of speculative, jealous voices from around her, a mocking wave of sound, and felt a humiliating blush crawl up her throat and colour her face.

Just as well, she told herself. Her clumsiness had broken the spell he'd cast over her, the magic he'd woven. This wasn't about her; it was about Annabel.

She turned to Lukas, and saw in his eyes an expression of gentle amusement.

'*Ça va?*' he asked, and Rhiannon tried to smile.

'Ummm…*ça va bien.*' Her rusty schoolgirl French to the rescue, she thought wryly.

But it obviously didn't impress him, for he smiled slightly and said, 'You're English.'

'Welsh, actually,' she admitted. 'I did a GCSE in French, but it's been a while.'

His smile deepened, his eyes lightened to the shimmering colour of dawn on the sea, and Rhiannon saw he had a dimple in his cheek.

'Can I get you a drink?' He was looking at her again in that assessing way, as if he were taking her in, deciding who she was. Considering his own reaction.

And she was considering hers—the way she leaned towards him, intuitively, a matter of instinct as well as desire. Every sense was humming, every nerve on high alert. When he looked at her in that warm, considering way, every thought in her mind seemed to vaporise. All she could do was feel.

'I'll have a white wine,' she said into the silence.

'Done.' He smiled, scattering her thoughts to the wind, and a glass of wine materialised before her. She took a grateful sip, letting the cool liquid zing pleasantly through her system. She put the glass down, turned to Lukas.

He was looking at her with expectation, yet also with something more. The languorous warmth of male appreciation, the treacherous heat of desire.

It thrilled her. It scared her.

It turned her mind to cotton, her bones to wax. Made her waver. Made her want.

Her mouth was dry, and she licked her lips. Tried to form a thought, a word. A sound.

'Are you here alone?' Lukas asked. His tone was one of polite interest, but his eyes were roaming her figure, stroking her as they flared with a heat Rhiannon felt flicker in her own core.

Could this actually be happening? Was Lukas Petrakides flirting with her? More than flirting; openly wanting. *Her.*

Her heart craved it, feared it. No, he couldn't be. Not him…not with a girl like her. A girl from nowhere, a girl with nothing.

Except a baby. His.

The reminder of Annabel's presence, her need, pulsed demandingly through Rhiannon's mind and heart.

That was why she was here…for Annabel. Only for Annabel.

'Yes, I'm alone,' she finally answered, her voice little more than a croak. She tried to gather her scattered wits and failed. She hadn't expected this reaction—treacherous, molten, overwhelming.

Real.

This was not part of her plan.

'You are?' He sounded surprised, and his gaze flicked over the crowd before coming to rest on her face with penetrating intensity. 'A holiday alone?' he clarified, and Rhiannon's blush deepened.

She really did sound pathetic. If he were flirting with her it had to be out of boredom or pity or both.

Except it didn't feel that way.

'Yes, although…' Now was the time to state her purpose. To mention Annabel.

Why was it the last thing she wanted to do?

'Although…?' he prompted. The matron on his right had left with a loud sniff, and Rhiannon could feel the speculative stares from the people around them.

They were wondering how a bourgeois bit-piece like her had

captured Lukas Petrakides's attention. She couldn't blame them—even if she didn't appreciate the contempt that was drawing like a palpable shroud around her. She was wondering the same thing herself.

'Nothing.' Coward.

'Ah.' There was a moment of silence, pregnant with possibility, heavy with intent. Rhiannon waited, too overwhelmed to speak, too affected to formulate more than a hazy thought…a need.

She didn't want him to go.

She wanted him.

It was ridiculous; it was real. Something pulsed to life between them—something Rhiannon couldn't even understand.

Lukas's mouth twisted in a smile, and he took a sip of wine. He looked undecided for a moment, vulnerably uncertain, and then resolve hardened his eyes, his face, his voice. 'It was nice chatting with you,' he said, and Rhiannon knew it was a dismissal.

For a moment she thought she saw regret shadow his eyes, but it was replaced with a formal cursory courtesy that she suspected was the expression with which he greeted everyone in the room.

If they'd shared a real moment, a connection, it was gone.

And so was her chance.

'Wait.' Lukas had already turned away, and Rhiannon was forced to scrabble at his sleeve. 'I need to say something to you.'

He turned. Hope lit his eyes for one wonderful moment. Rhiannon took a breath.

'I have something you need to hear.'

He stilled. The blank look returned, and suddenly it seemed dangerous.

'What would that be?'

Rhiannon took a breath. The desire she'd felt, the warmth, the connection, were distant memories. All she felt now was uncertainty. Fear. The cold, metallic tang was on her tongue. She was handling this wrong. She knew she was. But if Lukas would only listen to her, then he would understand.

He would accept, and he would be glad. She had to believe that.

'I think it would be better said in private.'

She spoke in a low voice, but still heard the shocked indrawn breaths from the gossipy vultures around her.

'You do?' His voice was soft, musing, but his eyes were as hard as steel.

She kept saying the wrong thing. She saw it in the way he looked at her now, with derision and dislike. What had happened? She didn't understand this world—its politics, its hidden agendas. She just wanted to tell him about his daughter.

'Yes…it is important, I promise. You need to know…' She trailed off uncertainly. She felt tension thrum in the air, in her body. In his.

There was a connection, but it wasn't a good one.

It felt very bad.

'I cannot imagine,' Lukas replied in a voice of lethal quiet, 'that you have anything to say to me that I need to know, Miss…?'

'Davies—Rhiannon Davies. And please believe me—I do. I only need a moment of your time…' And then a lifetime. But there would—please, God—be other opportunities to discuss their future. Annabel's future.

'I'm afraid I don't have a moment…for you,' Lukas said, his tone chillingly soft.

'No… No… Just wait…' She flung one hand out in appeal; it was ignored. 'You don't understand. Someone else is involved. We have a mutual friend.' Her words came out stilted, strained. Awful. Why hadn't she thought of a better way to handle this?

'I don't think we've ever met,' Lukas said after a tiny pause. 'And I doubt we have any mutual friends.'

They were from different worlds; it was glaringly obvious. He was accustomed to wealth, privilege, power—light years away from her small suburban existence in Wales.

He had power; she had nothing.

Except Annabel. The realisation gave her a much-needed boost of courage.

'No, we haven't met,' she agreed, meeting his gaze unflinchingly. 'But there is someone we both know—both care about. A friend…' Although, according to Leanne, she and Lukas had been a lot more than friendly.

For a moment Rhiannon's mind dwelt on that strangely unwelcome possibility—Lukas and Leanne, bodies entwined, fused. Lips, hips, shoulders, thighs. Passion created, enjoyed, shared. They'd made a child together.

She shook her head. She didn't want to think about it. Hadn't even asked Leanne about the details. A weekend of passion, Leanne had said with a sigh, before naming the father.

Take care of her for me. Don't let her down.

Love her.

That was what this was about. That was why she had come.

Annabel needed love. Real love. The love of her father.

'Someone we both care about?' Lukas repeated, and this time Rhiannon heard more of the steel. The incredulity. Her heart rate sped up, doubled. She nodded.

'Yes... And if you'd just give me a moment in private, I could explain. It would be...worth your while.'

He froze, and Rhiannon felt as if her heart had frozen as well. For a moment everything seemed suspended, still, that terrible moment before the storm hit and the lightning struck.

'Worth my while?' he repeated. It was a simple statement, yet it held a wealth of unpleasant meaning. Alarm prickled along Rhiannon's spine, tingling up her nape as Lukas made eye contact with someone over her shoulder. Something was happening. Something bad.

He gave a brief, almost indiscernible nod, then his icy gaze snapped back to her—unyielding, unmerciful.

She suppressed a shiver.

Had she actually thought this was a gentle man?

'I'm just trying to be polite,' she explained. 'By requesting some privacy—'

'I can be polite,' he replied with silky, lethal intent. 'As a courtesy, I'm letting you know that you have five seconds before my security guards escort you from this room and this resort.'

Shock shot through her, followed by scathing disbelief and, worse, hurt. She should have expected this, but she hadn't. After that first moment she'd thought he might be kind.

Different.

She'd believed what the tabloids said—the image of the man they exalted.

She was a fool.

'You're making a mistake.'

'I don't think so.'

'Please…I don't want anything from you—at least nothing that you wouldn't be prepared to give—' She grabbed his hand; he removed it with distaste.

'Is that so? Because I'm prepared to give you nothing. Goodbye, Miss Davies.'

Before Rhiannon could form a reply, one last appeal, a hand clamped none too gently on her arm.

'This way, miss.'

He was kicking her out! Humiliated fury washed through her in sickening waves as the security guard tugged her firmly from her stool. She stumbled to her feet, threw a hand out to the bar to steady herself.

Lukas Petrakides watched impassively with cool grey eyes.

Rhiannon hated him then.

'You can't do this,' she said in a furious whisper, and he raised one eyebrow.

'Then you don't know me very well.'

'I don't want to know you! I want to *talk* to you!'

The guard was tugging her backwards, and Rhiannon was forced to follow him, stumbling, while a murmur of curious whispers and titters followed her, surrounded her in a mocking chorus.

Lukas watched, arms folded, eyes hard, expression flat.

This was her last chance. Her only hope.

'You have a baby!' she shouted, and was rewarded with a ripple of shocked murmurs in the crowd and a look of stunned disbelief on Lukas's face before she was pulled through the doorway and out of sight.

CHAPTER TWO

YOU have a baby.

Lukas barely registered the din of speculative gossip that rang out around him. Someone spoke to him, an excited jabber. He merely shrugged before forcing himself to reply politely.

You have a baby.

Absurd. Impossible. The woman was a liar.

He knew that—knew she was just another common blackmailer, a petty thief looking for a handout.

He'd seen them, dealt with them before. He'd recognised the patter as soon as she'd started, the female flattery disguising the threat underneath.

Mutual friends. Something he needed to hear.

Hardly.

He just didn't understand why he felt so disappointed.

Last night, when he'd seen her on the beach, he'd felt a connection. And then when she'd shown up at the reception, met his gaze, walked towards him with a smile that was tender, uncertain and yet filled with promise, he'd felt it again. Deep, real, alive.

False. All he'd felt was cheap, easy desire. Lust masquerading as need.

His disappointment was no more than he deserved for giving in to desire for something—someone—for even a moment.

Wanting was weakness. Desire was dangerous. He'd seen the shameful results, lived with them every day.

He had responsibilities, duties, and those were what counted. What mattered.

Nothing else did.

Nothing else could.

He knew the drill: his guards would take her to a discreet office kept for just this purpose, make her sign a gagging order, and show her the door.

He'd never see her again.

Yet suddenly he wanted to know. Needed to know just what her game was—what information she pretended to have, what she hoped to get.

Then he'd forget her completely.

'Excuse me… *Pardon…*' He repeated the phrase in several languages as the crowd mingled and jostled for his attention, moving past everyone with firm decision.

He pushed through the double doors, strode down the corridor towards the lobby.

What had she expected? That he would believe her dirty little tale and cut her a cheque? He shook his head slowly, disbelief and fury pouring through him, scalding his soul.

Had she been planning her little manoeuvre last night, on the beach? Was there someone else involved? Some man waiting greedily back in their hotel room?

Or was she playing another game? Selling her story to a tabloid? The gossip rags had so little dirt to dish on him, it wouldn't surprise him if they were paying people to make it up.

He strode into the lobby, heard the flutter of greeting from an army of receptionists and ignored them, making for the small office, its door discreetly tucked behind a potted palm in one corner of the spacious room.

He paused outside the door, listening. Waiting to hear what ridiculous tale she would spin.

'I don't want money!' He heard her furious denial, shook his head. What was she playing for? A bigger bribe?

'Sign this statement, Miss Davies.' Tony, one of his two security guards, spoke with weary patience. 'By signing it you agree not to sell or disclose any information regarding Mr Petrakides, the Petrakides family, or Petrakides Properties. Then you will leave this resort. Petrakides Properties will pay for one night's accommodation in a local hotel as redress. Your belongings will be sent there this evening.'

Lukas heard the silence through the door, felt her incredulity, her fury, her fear. His hand rested on the knob.

'That's not possible.' Her voice was a whisper, with a thread of steel through its core.

'It is in every way possible,' Tony replied flatly. 'And as soon as you sign the statement, it will be put into effect.'

'I'll sign the statement,' Rhiannon replied with barely a waver. 'But you *cannot* throw me out of this resort. There is a baby in my hotel room, and that child belongs to Lukas Petrakides!'

Lukas's hand tightened on the knob as shock and outrage battled for precedence. Had the lying slut actually brought a baby as proof? Used an innocent child in her despicable scheme? It was vile. He should have her arrested, prosecuted...

The Petrakides family's policy, however, was to remove any instigators as quickly and quietly as possible. Prosecution, in this case, was not an option.

For a brief moment Lukas imagined his father's reaction when the tabloids printed the story about his so-called child. He knew someone at the party would dish the goods.

His mouth tightened; his heart hardened. She wasn't worth the trouble she'd put him to.

'If that is so,' Lukas's security guard said after a tiny, tense pause, 'then I will escort you to your hotel room to collect this child. Then you will go.'

There was a silence. When her voice came out, however, it shocked him. It was small and sad and defeated.

'You have this all wrong,' Rhiannon said. 'I don't want to blackmail anyone—least of all Lukas Petrakides. I simply have reason to believe his daughter is in my care, and I thought he should know that...know her.' This last came out in a sorry, aching whisper that created an answering throb in Lukas's mid-section. His gut, not his heart.

She was sincere, even if she was mistaken. Or she was a phe-nomenal actress. He forced himself not to care. Then he shook his head slowly. She had to be acting, faking. How on earth she could possibly believe she had his child when he had never seen her before—what could she be playing at?

Still he paused. Wondered. Wanted to know.

And he realised with damning weakness—need—that he wanted to see her again.

He turned the knob.

Rhiannon choked back a scream of frustration and defeat. This had gone so horribly, horribly wrong. No one believed her; no one even cared.

From Lukas Petrakides down, all she'd come up against were blank walls of indifference, unconcern. They didn't care what she had to say, what truth there might be to her tale.

They wanted her gone.

'I don't want money,' she repeated, for what felt like the hun-dredth time. 'I just want a moment alone with Mr Petrakides to explain. That's *all*.'

'So you've said before, Miss Davies,' the guard told her in a bored voice, clearly unimpressed.

'Then why don't you believe me?' Rhiannon snapped, but the security guard had gone silent, his gaze on the door.

She turned, her breath coming out in a sudden, surprised rush when she saw Lukas Petrakides standing there. He leaned against the doorframe, one hand thrust into the pocket of his dark grey trousers, the other braced against the wall.

She hadn't heard him come in, yet how could she ever have been unaware of his presence? He filled the space, took the air. She sucked in a much needed breath, tried to gather her scattered wits and courage.

Lukas flicked her with a cool, impassive gaze even as he ad-dressed the guards.

'I'll deal with this.'

The two men filed out of the room without a word.

Rhiannon watched, sickened by the blatant display of power. *Abuse* of power. Lukas was a man who expected obedience— total, absolute, unquestioning.

She was so out of her depth, over her head, and it scared her. Yet this was Annabel's father.

They were alone in the small room, and she was conscious of her own ragged breathing, her pounding heart. His eyes flicked over her in cool and clearly unimpressed assessment.

'You have a child in your hotel room?' he asked in a detached voice, as if it were of little interest.

'Yes…yours.'

'I see.' His smile was cold, mocking, a parody. 'When did we conceive this child, I wonder?'

Shock drenched her in icy, humiliating waves as she realised the assumption he'd so easily—and obviously—made. He really did think she was a liar. 'Annabel's not mine!'

'Annabel. A girl?'

'Yes.'

'Whose child is she, then? Besides mine, of course.'

'Leanne Weston. You…you met her at a club in London, took her to Naxos.' She felt silly repeating information he must already know—but perhaps he needed clarification? Perhaps, despite his reputation, there had been women? Many women?

The thought made her stomach roil unpleasantly.

He raised his eyebrows in surprised interest. 'I did? Ah, yes. Naxos. Beautiful place. Did we have fun?'

Rhiannon gritted her teeth. 'I couldn't say, but from Leanne's description you were certainly busy!'

'And why is she not here herself?' Lukas questioned silkily. 'I'd recognise her, of course. Perhaps I'd even recall our dirty little weekend. Or would you prefer that I do not see the woman who supposedly bore my child? Maybe I wouldn't recognise her after all?' The derisive lilt to his voice made Rhiannon grit her teeth.

'If Leanne were able to be here, I hope she would be,' she said, her nerves taut, fraying, ready to split apart. 'Although after your weekend affair she was pragmatic enough to realise it was over. You never gave her your phone number, or attempted to contact her.' Frustration rose within her, clamoured into a silent howl in her throat. 'But this is nonsense to talk like this. I don't care about what you did with Leanne in Naxos. What I care about is your daughter, and I should think that's what you would care about too.'

'Ah, yes, my daughter. This Annabel.' He folded his arms, smiled with the stealthy confidence of a predator. And Rhiannon was the prey. 'You brought her here? To the hotel?'

'Yes…'

'I suppose you thought the added embarrassment of an actual child on the premises would increase your pay-off?'

'My what?' Rhiannon shook her head. Did he still think she wanted to blackmail him? Was that what this horrible little interrogation was about? 'I don't want your money,' she said tightly. 'As I've said before. I just wanted you to *know*.'

'How kind of you. So now that I know, we can say goodbye. Correct?' His cool eyes suddenly blazed silver with challenge; Rhiannon felt a hollow pit open inside her—a pit to drown in.

She'd come to France to find not just Lukas Petrakides, but a man who would love Annabel openly, wholly, unconditionally.

The way fathers did.

The way they were supposed to.

She should have realised what a fantasy that was.

'I thought you were a man of responsibility,' she said in a choked whisper. 'A man of honour.'

Lukas stilled, his eyes darkening dangerously. 'I am. That is precisely why I'm not going to pay you to keep silent about your little brat!'

'*Your* brat, if you choose to use such terms,' Rhiannon flashed, wounded to her core by his nasty words, his brutal assessment. He was talking about his own *child*. She shook her head. 'I don't understand how a man like you—a man like the papers claim you are—cannot care one iota for your own flesh and blood. I thought…' She shook her head slowly, realisation dawning with painful intensity and awareness.

'You thought what?' he demanded flatly, and she looked up at him with wide, guileless eyes.

'I thought it would be different because she was yours.' It came out as a wretched whisper, a confession. An aching realisation that a dream she'd cherished and clung to for so long was in fact false. Rhiannon didn't know what hurt more—the current reality or the faded memory. Annabel's past or her own. 'I thought you would care.'

He stared at her for a moment, his mouth tightening in impatience. 'But you *know,* Miss Davies, that this is a fabrication. I don't know who dreamed up your sordid little scheme—whether it was you or your suspiciously absent friend Leanne—but we both know I did not father the child that is in your hotel room.'

Rhiannon stared at him in disbelief. 'But you…you said you were in Naxos!'

'I may have visited my family's resort in Naxos,' he agreed with stinging clarity. 'But I did not take your friend—or any other woman there—and I certainly did not father a child.'

'But Leanne said—'

'She lied. As you are lying.'

'No.' Rhiannon shook her head. 'No. She didn't lie. And neither did I. She was so certain…she spoke of you so warmly…'

He made a sound of impatient disgust. 'I'm flattered.'

'But how do you know? How can you be sure?' She gulped down her own uncertainties, the fears clamouring within her, threatening to spill over in a scream of denial, of desperation. Everything had been turned upside down by this revelation.

Rhiannon had never doubted Leanne's word. Never. There had been no reason to—no reason for her friend to lie. Now she wondered if she should have questioned. Doubted. If Leanne, for some inexplicable reason, *had* lied. It would be a terrible deception. And for what purpose?

But, no… When Leanne had named Lukas Petrakides as the father of her child she'd been so certain, so…*appreciative.*

Wistful. The memory, for Leanne, had been sweet. There had been nothing calculating or deceptive about her explanation—and why should there have been?

She'd been dying.

'How do I *know?*' Lukas raised one eyebrow, as if daring her to make him answer such a question.

'I mean…' Rhiannon felt humiliating colour flood her face. 'There must have been women…' She assumed, despite his un-sullied reputation, that there still were women. There were always women. Attractive, wealthy, discreet, willing to give and receive pleasure—satisfy a need.

'Ah.' His smile was mocking, bittersweet. 'But there you're wrong, Miss Davies. There have been no women. Not for two years.'

His face remained impassive even as Rhiannon gaped in shock. She wasn't sure why she should find this so surprising; *she* hadn't slept with anyone in the last two years. Or, for that matter, ever.

Lukas Petrakides, however, exuded raw strength, powerful virility. The idea that he'd gone without women—without *sex*—for such a length of time seemed ludicrous. Impossible.

Men like him thrived on passion…needed it. Didn't they?

Was Lukas really different? Was he gay? The thought was absurd. Cold, then…? Although there seemed nothing cold about him.

Was he just incredibly restrained?

After her mind had stopped whirling she realised with cold, stark clarity just what this meant.

Annabel couldn't possibly be Lukas's child.

She'd come here for nothing.

'Are you…sure?' she asked, her voice a rusty croak. Yet she knew what an inane question it was—just as she knew he was telling the truth. In some bizarre, inexplicable way, she trusted him. Trusted his word.

'I don't forget such things. If there was any possibility of course I would have a paternity test taken. If the child were indeed mine I would care for it. Naturally.'

Rhiannon shook her head. She didn't want to believe it. Didn't want to consider the utter waste of her travelling to France, spending far more money than she ever should have on a hotel and, worse, losing any hope of a better life for Annabel.

Lukas Petrakides was not Annabel's father. Rhiannon stared, her mind forming one impossible denial after another. She wanted to cry. To cry for Annabel, for herself.

For lost dreams of the father-daughter reunion she'd been dreaming of for years.

It was never going to happen.

But she wasn't going to cry.

'I'm sorry your little charade didn't pay off,' Lukas said with a cold smile. 'But at least you can be thankful that I won't press charges. You and your…prop will vacate the premises within the next fifteen minutes.'

'My prop?' Rhiannon repeated blankly, before she realised he was talking about a person. A child. Annabel. 'You still think this is a blackmail attempt?' She shook her head, surprised at the rush of relief that Annabel would not be tied to a man who thought so little of her, of humanity. 'Why can't you believe I came here with your interests—Annabel's interests—at heart? I didn't come for money, Mr Petrakides. I came to find Annabel a father.'

'Charming.' Lukas's eyes were flat, cold and hard. 'Since you didn't, you can leave.'

Rhiannon knew he didn't believe her, and she forced herself not to care. She didn't need to impress Lukas Petrakides; she was out of his life, and so was Annabel.

Yet it still hurt.

She straightened her shoulders, lifted her chin. 'Fine. I'm sorry I wasted your time.'

Lukas jerked his head in the semblance of a nod. Rhiannon forced herself to continue, even though she didn't want to accept anything from this man…to need anything from him.

'You mentioned another hotel as redress? Could I have the details, please?' Colour scorched her cheeks. If she'd had any money left she wouldn't have asked, but she was desperate, and they needed a place to stay until their flight tomorrow.

'The information will be at the front desk by the time you leave.'

'Thank you.' Stiff with dignity, her legs trembling, she walked out of the room. Lukas's eyes seemed to burn into her back.

She wouldn't cry. She wouldn't. She was stronger than that. Tougher. In all the years of loneliness, disappointment, and grief, her eyes had remained dry. They would remain so now.

Lukas watched her go, his lips twisting in a mocking smile. She'd given up quite easily when she realised he wasn't playing ball. She was obviously an amateur at the blackmail game—as was this mysterious Leanne.

Had they honestly thought they could pin something on him—*him*, Lukas Petrakides? That he would bow to their outrageous demands?

Something pricked him, pricked his conscience, and he realised with a jolt of uncomfortable surprise what it was. Guilt.

Why should he feel guilty?

Because she so obviously didn't want your money. She hadn't actually asked for a single euro.

Had he assumed the worst?

He shook his head. The baby wasn't his, and the friend Leanne had to have been lying. She'd have to know she hadn't slept with him!

And yet…what if Rhiannon hadn't known?

What if she'd been duped?

Lukas hesitated; he didn't like uncertainty. He didn't like not knowing.

So, he decided grimly, he would find out.

Rhiannon's mind was numb as she paid off the babysitter and began packing her paltry possessions. Annabel was asleep in the travel cot, one arm flung above her head, her breath coming in soft little sighs.

Rhiannon gazed down at her sleeping form with a mixture of

longing and desperation. What now? What future could they have? What future could she offer this child?

'I tried,' she whispered as she gently touched one chubby fist. 'I really tried.'

'Whose child is that really, Miss Davies?'

The harsh voice had her whirling around. Lukas stood in the doorway, his face composed, closed. Cold.

'How did you get in?' she demanded, and he shrugged.

'I own the hotel, Miss Davies. I can enter whichever room I please.'

'It's a violation of privacy—'

'If anyone is going to speak of violation, it should be me,' he replied. 'Whose child is that?'

'Not yours, apparently,' Rhiannon snapped. 'And you don't need to know anything else. You're not involved, Mr. Petrakides, as you were kind enough to remind me.' She turned away, stuffing her belongings into the cheap suitcase.

He watched, nonplussed. Rhiannon was conscious of the mess of the room: the spill of cosmetics by the bathroom sink, a bra hanging on the back of the chair. She grabbed the garment and stuffed it in the bag, saw how Lukas's lips quirked in a rueful smile.

She glared at him. 'Why are you here?'

In response he moved closer to the cot and studied Annabel.

'This Leanne is the mother?' he asked after a moment.

'I told you she was!' Rhiannon replied in exasperation. What was he playing at? Why did he care now?

'And you really believed her?' Lukas continued slowly. 'That she had an affair...with me?'

Rhiannon paused. He sounded different—as if he might believe she actually wasn't in on the so-called scam. 'She had no reason to lie,' she said after a moment. In her mind she could picture Leanne's wasted body, hear the cough that had racked her thin frame.

'Didn't she?' There was a cynical edge to his voice that Rhiannon didn't like. 'Surely,' he continued, turning away from Annabel, 'you must realise that she was hoping for this exact situation? Even if I didn't acknowledge the child—which she no doubt expects—I might be willing to cut a generous cheque to keep this unfortunate episode from reaching the press. I guard my reputation very closely, Miss Davies, as you undoubtedly know. Where is this Leanne now? Waiting nearby? Or back in Wales?'

Rhiannon could only stare, her mind whirling at the bleak, base picture he'd painted.

'No, she's not waiting for anything,' she said finally, unable to meet his incredulous, derisive look. 'She's dead.'

The events of the last two weeks danced crazily before her eyes—Leanne's arrival on her doorstep, her rapid descent to death, guardianship thrust upon Rhiannon without any warning. How could she explain such a chain of fantastic events to Lukas Petrakides? To anyone? It would sound made up; he wouldn't believe her. He would think it was just part of some nefarious blackmailing scheme.

She let out a wild hiccup of laughter, her arms wrapping around herself as a matter of self-protection. Self-denial.

Lukas muttered something under his breath, then moved towards her. 'Why don't you sit down?' Before Rhiannon could protest, he pushed her onto the edge of the bed. His hands burned her skin through the thin fabric of her blouse. She felt their warmth and strength like a brand.

'You're in shock,' he stated flatly, rummaging in the room's minibar and coming up with a small plastic bottle filled with a clear liquid.

'I'm not in shock,' she protested, even as her insides wobbled and rebelled. 'I'm…I'm *sad.*' She knew it sounded pathetic; she could tell Lukas thought so too by the way he raked her with one uncomprehending glance.

He wouldn't understand, of course. He didn't care about Annabel, and he probably wondered why she seemed to. Rhiannon closed her eyes.

She'd only known the baby two weeks. She still hadn't quite figured out how to hold her, and bottle feedings were awkward. The nappies she put on fell off half of the time. She wasn't used to infants, to their noise and dribble. Yet she loved her. At least, she knew she *would* love her, if she was given the chance.

If she let herself have the chance.

She'd known from the moment Leanne named Lukas Petrakides as the father that she would give Annabel up if she needed to. If he wanted her to.

And she'd hoped he would…for Annabel's sake. Annabel's happiness.

Lukas poured the liquid into a glass and put it into her hand. Her fingers closed around it and she opened her eyes.

'Drink.'

She squinted dubiously at the glass and drank. Only to promptly splutter it all over the carpet—and Lukas's shoes.

'What is that stuff?' she exclaimed, wiping her mouth with the back of her hand. Her throat burned all the way to her gut, which churned in rebellion.

'Brandy. You've never had it, I take it?'

'No.' Rhiannon gazed up at him resentfully. 'You could have warned me.'

Lukas took out a handkerchief and handed it to her. 'It was for the shock.'

'I told you I wasn't in shock!'

'No? You just looked as if you were about to faint.'

'Thanks very much!' Rhiannon's eyes blazed even as hectic, humiliated colour flushed her face. She lowered her voice for Annabel's sake, and it came out in a resentful hiss. 'I admit the last fortnight has been a bit crazy. I have every right to look pale.'

She struggled upwards, for control, only to have him place his hands on her shoulders and push her gently, firmly back down onto the bed.

'Sit down.'

His palms were flat against her breastbone, his fingers curling around her shoulders. Suddenly everything was different. The hostility in the room was replaced with a tension of a completely different kind.

Desire.

Rhiannon gasped at his sudden touch, at the rush of surprised feeling it caused within her.

Lukas's mouth flickered in a smile—a sardonic, knowing curve of his lips. His head was bent towards hers, his face inches from her own. Her eyes traced the hard line of his mouth, a mouth with lips as full and soft and kissable as an angel's.

Some angel. Lukas Petrakides, with his dark hair and countenance, looked more like a demon than a cherub. But he was a handsome devil at that. And dangerous.

Her whole body burned with awareness of this man—his body, his presence, his scent. He smelled of pine and soap, a simple fragrance that made her inhale. Ache. Want.

He looked down at her for a moment, regret and wonder chasing across his face, darkening his eyes to iron. His hands were still on her shoulders, tantalisingly close to her breasts, which seemed to ache and strain towards him, towards his touch.

What would it be like to kiss him? To feel those sculpted lips against hers, to caress that lean jaw? Rhiannon's face flamed. She was sure her thoughts and her desire were obvious. She could feel the hunger in her own eyes.

She tried to look away. And failed.

This was about Annabel.

Her mind screeched a halt to her careening heart, and she dragged in a desperate breath.

This wasn't about her—her need to be touched. Loved.

'No…' It came out as a shaky whisper, a word that begged to be disbelieved. 'Don't.'

Lukas stilled, then dropped his hands from her shoulders.

Rhiannon felt bereft, empty. Stupid. A moment of desire, intense as it was, was only that. A moment.

A connection. He stood up, raked a hand through his hair. The room was silent save for their breathing, uneven and ragged, and Annabel's little sighs.

She hiccuped in her sleep, and Lukas turned, startled. He'd forgotten the baby—as she had, for one damning moment.

'We don't want to wake her up,' he said after a moment. 'Come outside.' He opened the sliding glass door that led outside.

The beach in front of the hotel room was private, separate from the crowded public area and blissfully quiet.

Rhiannon kicked off her heels and dug her toes in the cool, white sand. The sun was starting to sink in an azure sky, a blazing trail of light shimmering on the surface of the water.

It was the late afternoon of a day that had gone on for ever.

'What has happened in the last fortnight?' Lukas finally asked, his face averted.

She shook her head, tried to focus. 'Leanne—Annabel's mother—was a childhood friend of mine,' she began stiltedly, words and phrases whirling through her mind. None seemed to fit, to explain the sheer impossibility and desperation of Leanne's situation. Of her own situation. Where to begin? How to explain?

Why would he care?

Why had he come back?

'And?' Lukas prompted, his voice edged with a bite of impatience. His hands were on his hips, his powerful shoulders thrown back, grey eyes assessing. Calculating.

Rhiannon looked up; her vision was blurred. She blinked quickly, almost wanting another sip of that terrible brandy to steady her nerves. Shock them into numbness, at least.

'She came to me after she'd been diagnosed with lung cancer and asked me to be Annabel's guardian. She only had a few weeks to live. She'd lived hard already, so she didn't seem that surprised. She told me she'd never expected to live long.'

'A waste of a life.' It was a brutal, if accurate, assessment.

'To be fair to Leanne,' Rhiannon said quietly, 'she didn't have much to live for. She was a foster child, shipped from one family to the next. She'd always been a bit wild, and when she came to live in our little town in Wales, well…' She shrugged. 'There wasn't much room for a girl like Leanne. People tried to reach out to her at first, but I don't…I don't think she understood how to accept love. She pushed everyone away, grew wilder and wilder, and eventually no one wanted her around any more.'

'Yet you were her friend?'

'Yes…but not a very good one.' Rhiannon felt a familiar pang of guilt deep inside. She could have done more, helped more. Yet the needs of her own family had taken precedence; they always had. 'We lost touch after school,' she admitted, after a moment when they had both seemed lost in their own separate thoughts. 'I never bothered to try and reconnect.'

'Yet she came to you when she was dying, to care for her child?' Lukas raised an eyebrow in obvious scepticism.

'I was the only person she trusted enough to care for Annabel,' Rhiannon said simply. 'There was no one else. There never had been.' The realisation made her ache. It was also the leaden weight of responsibility that rested heavily on her shoulders, her heart.

She would not let Leanne down.

She would not let Annabel down.

She saw Lukas's eyes narrow, his mouth tighten, and realised with an uncomfortable twinge that she was wasting his time. He should be at the reception, meeting and greeting, drinking and laughing.

Flirting.

'But this has nothing to do with you,' she said. 'As you have already made abundantly clear.' She shook her head. 'Why are you here?'

Lukas was silent for a moment, his eyes, his face, his tone all hard. Dark. 'Because I'm afraid it may have something to do with me,' he said finally, 'after all.'

'What? Are you saying…you did…?'

'No, of course not.' Lukas waved a hand in impatient dismissal. 'I don't lie, Miss Davies.'

'Neither do I,' Rhiannon flashed, but he merely flung out one hand—an imperious command for her to still her words, her movements.

His fingers, she saw, were long, lean and brown, tapering to clean, square nails. It was a hand that radiated both strength and grace.

She gave herself a mental shake; it was just a *hand*.

Why did he affect her so much? Why did she let him?

Was she just so desperate for someone—anyone—to want her? To want Annabel.

'I'd like you to tell me how Leanne came to mention my name. After the little stunt you pulled at the reception, the tabloids will be filled with stories about my secret love-child.' His face twisted in a grimace, and Rhiannon flinched. 'I want to know all the facts.'

'I wouldn't have said anything if you'd listened,' Rhiannon snapped, unrepentant. 'Instead of assuming some sordid black-mail story—'

'Just tell me, Miss Davies.' He spoke coldly, and Rhiannon realised that even though he'd returned, even though he'd shown a moment of compassion, of understanding, he still didn't believe her. Didn't trust her.

She drew in a wavering breath. 'I told you. She said she met you at a club in London. You took her to Naxos. To be honest…' She looked up at him with frank eyes. 'The man she described was younger than you are—a bit more…debonair, I suppose.'

He raised his eyebrows, his mouth curving in mock outrage. 'You don't think I'm debonair?'

The humour in his voice, in his eyes, surprised her. Warmed her. Rhiannon found she was smiling back in wry apology. It felt good to smile. It eased the pain in her heart. 'It's not that…' She could hardly explain the difference between the man before her and the man Leanne had described.

Her friend's glowing phrases had been indications to Rhiannon of a player—a man who lived life full and hard, just as Leanne had. The descriptions of Lukas Petrakides in the press hadn't matched up, but Rhiannon had been prepared to believe that the man with the sterling reputation had enjoyed one moment—well, one weekend—of weakness. Of pleasure.

She hadn't blamed him for it. It had made him seem more human. More approachable.

'She discovered she was pregnant several weeks later,' she finished. 'By that time she'd lost contact with you. She realised it had only been a weekend fling.'

'Something she was used to, apparently?'

'Don't judge her!' Rhiannon's eyes flashed angry amber as she looked up at him. 'You never knew her, and you don't know what it's like to live a life where no one cares what happens to you. Leanne had no one. *No one*,' she emphasised. 'She was just looking for a little love.'

'And she found a *little*,' Lukas agreed tersely. 'Did she try to get in touch with the father?'

She shook her head. 'No, she didn't see the point. She was sad, of course, but pragmatic enough to realise that a man like—like you wouldn't be interested in supporting her or her illegitimate child.'

'Surely she could have used the money?'

Rhiannon shrugged. 'She was proud, in her own way. It had been clear from the outset that it was a weekend fling. I suppose,' she added slowly, 'she didn't want to be rejected by someone…again. At least this was on her own terms.'

Pity flickered across his face, shadowed his eyes. 'A sad life,' he said quietly, and Rhiannon nodded, her throat tight.

'Yes.'

'So Annabel's own mother didn't bother notifying the father of her child, but you did?'

Rhiannon met his gaze directly. 'Yes.'

'Why come all this way? Why not call?'

'I tried. Your receptionist led me to believe you wouldn't get my messages. And you didn't, did you?'

Lukas shrugged. 'I'm an important man, Miss Davies. I receive too many messages, solicitations.'

'No doubt.' She didn't bother to hide the contempt in her voice. 'Too important to consider your own daughter.'

'She's not mine.'

'Then why are you here?' Rhiannon demanded. 'Why did you come back? Did you suddenly conveniently remember that you *did* go to Naxos after all?'

His eyes blazed silver—an electric look that sizzled between them so that Rhiannon took an involuntary step back.

'I told you I did not lie.'

Rhiannon believed him. So why was he here? What did he want?

'You took the chance,' Lukas continued, 'that I would want to know this child, and no doubt support it.'

'I didn't come here for money,' Rhiannon snapped. 'As I believe I've said before.'

'Not blackmail money,' Lukas replied, unfazed by her anger. 'Maintenance. If this Annabel were indeed my child, you would certainly be within your rights to think that I would support her financially.'

Rhiannon was disconcerted by his flat, businesslike tone. Was it all about money to people like him? 'That's true,' she agreed carefully. 'But that isn't why I came. If I'd just wanted money I would have filed a court order. I came because I believe children should know their parents. If there was any chance you might love your daughter—that you might *want* her...' Her voice wavered dangerously and she gulped back the emotion that threatened to rise up in a tide of regret and sorrow. 'I had to take that chance.' She didn't want to reveal so much to Lukas, to a man who regarded her as if she were a problem to be resolved, an annoyance to be dealt with.

Lukas stared at her, his eyes narrowed, yet filled with the cold light of comprehension. He looked as though he'd finally figured it out, and he scorned the knowledge.

'You didn't come for money,' he said slowly, almost to himself. 'You came for freedom.'

'I told you—'

'To give this baby away,' he finished flatly, and every word was a condemnation, a judgement.

'I want to do what's best for Annabel!' Rhiannon protested, her voice turning shrill. '*Whatever* that is.'

'A convenient excuse,' he dismissed.

Rhiannon clenched her fists, fury boiling through her. Yet mixed with it was guilt. There was a shred of truth in Lukas's assessment. She had been prepared to give Annabel up...but only because it was the right thing to do.

It had to be.

'There's no need for this,' she said in a steely voice. 'So why don't you just go? And so will I.' She turned back to the sliding glass door.

'No one is going anywhere.'

The command was barked out so harshly that Rhiannon stopped, stiffened from shock. 'Excuse me?'

'You will not go,' Lukas told her shortly. 'This matter has not been resolved.'

'This matter,' Rhiannon retorted, 'has nothing to do with you!'

'It has everything to do with me,' he replied grimly, 'since you have involved me in such a public way. You won't leave until I've had some answers.' He paused, reining in his temper with obvious effort. 'Answers you've been looking for too, perhaps?'

Rhiannon glared at him, but she didn't move. He was right, she knew. He *was* involved now, and that was her fault. She owed him a few more minutes of her time at least.

'Why do you think your friend lied?' he asked abruptly.

Rhiannon shrugged. 'I don't know. That's why I didn't think she *had* lied—she'd no reason. She was dying. I thought she'd want me to know Annabel's father, even if she never intended for me to get in touch with him.'

'She told you not to?'

'No, she didn't say anything about that. She just...' She swallowed, forced herself to continue. 'She just asked me to care for her. Love her.' Her throat ached and she looked down.

'A mother's dying request?'

Rhiannon couldn't tell if he was being snide or not. She gulped. 'Yes.' She looked up at him. 'She had nothing to gain by lying. I honestly think she believed she was with Lukas Petrakides...with you.'

Lukas stiffened, his expression becoming like that of a predator that had scented danger. There was no fear, only awareness.

'But we both know it wasn't me.' His mouth twisted wryly, but there was a hard edge of bitter realisation in his eyes. 'So it had to have been someone else...someone who told her my name.'

Rhiannon shook her head in confusion. 'Who would do that?'

Lukas muttered an expletive in Greek under his breath. 'I should have considered it,' he said, his face hardening into resolve. 'He's done it before.'

Rhiannon felt as if she were teetering on the edge of a dangerous precipice. She didn't want to look down, didn't want to cross over. She just wanted to tiptoe quietly away.

'Who are you talking about?' she asked faintly, and when Lukas met her gaze his face was full of grim realisation.

'My nephew.'

CHAPTER THREE

'YOUR nephew?' Rhiannon stared at him in blank incredulity. He looked angry, determined. Hard. 'But how...? I mean why...?'

She'd come here with the assumption—the *belief*—that Lukas Petrakides was Annabel's father. A man of integrity, honour, responsibility. A man who would love her.

She wasn't prepared for alternatives.

She didn't want them.

'Why would your nephew use your name?' she finally asked as Lukas continued to stare, arms folded, his expression implacable. 'Who is he, anyway?'

'My nephew, Christos Stefanos, has used my name before.' Lukas stared out at the shifting colours of the sea—blue, green, scarlet and orange in the setting sun. 'I think he might have used it again with your friend. He's twenty-two, wild, irresponsible, unscrupulous,' he continued in a flat tone. 'He often travels to London—his mother, my sister Antonia, lives there. He could very well have met your Leanne in some club there, flown her to Naxos on a whim, and discarded her after a weekend. It is,' he finished with scathing emphasis, 'entirely within his character to do so.'

Rhiannon's thoughts were flying, whirling round and round in frightened, desperate circles. Lukas Petrakides as Annabel's father was one thing. He was known to be steady, responsible. A good father figure. That was why she had come.

This Christos was something else entirely.

'But why?' she asked again, clutching at one seemingly improbable thread.

'To impress your friend?' Lukas shrugged. 'Or more likely to annoy me. He likes to give me bad press, although the tabloid journalists are wise to him by now. They usually ignore his little peccadilloes.'

'But surely people—the press—would know he wasn't you?'

Lukas's mouth twisted in harsh acknowledgement. 'I keep a low profile. There are few photographs of me, and Christos has a family resemblance. He only does it outside of Greece—he knows he can't get away with it there.' He sighed, raking a hand through his hair. 'It has been an annoyance in the past, but now it poses…'

'A major inconvenience?' Rhiannon finished, and he gave her a cool look.

'A challenge, certainly.'

Rhiannon was silent for a moment. Her thoughts chased themselves down dark tunnels that led to implications her heart shied away from. There was too much new information. Too much to think about…to wonder about. To be frightened about.

'From the sound of him, I don't think he would make a good father,' she finally said. 'Would he?'

Lukas was ominously silent. 'I cannot say he is particularly suited for the role.'

'Or interested in it?' Rhiannon surmised, feeling sick. She'd come to France to find Annabel's father…but not this. Not some young, rakish sot who couldn't care less. Not someone who would openly reject her.

'No, probably not,' Lukas agreed after a tense moment.

'He won't want Annabel,' she said in a hollow voice. 'Will he?'

Lukas's expression was like steel. Flint. 'No,' he said flatly. 'He won't.'

Rhiannon shook her head. This was so far from what she'd hoped. Dreamed. She realised now that the happily-ever-after she'd been planning in her head was a fantasy, pathetic and unreal. Could she leave Annabel with a man who didn't want her?

Could she take her home?

Nothing made sense. Nothing felt right.

'What are you going to do?' Rhiannon asked. She didn't like giving control to Lukas, no matter how used to it he was. She just didn't know what to do next.

Lukas was studying her in an odd way, his mouth twisting in a grimace of acknowledgement. 'You really don't want her,' he stated flatly. 'That's why you came, isn't it? To give her up...to anyone willing to take her.'

'If that were true,' Rhiannon snapped, 'I would have left her with Social Services. Don't mistake me, Mr Petrakides. I have Annabel's best interests at heart.'

'Undoubtedly.' It came out as a sneer.

Rhiannon shook her head. If Lukas wanted to judge her for giving up a child she couldn't truly call her own—if he thought her attempt to find Annabel's father was suspect—then fine. She refused to exonerate herself. She didn't need to.

'If Annabel is indeed Christos's child,' Lukas stated with flat finality, 'then she is my great-niece. My relative.' In case she didn't yet get it, he added with steely determination, 'My responsibility.'

'I see.' Rhiannon thought of every article she'd read, every glowing word about Lukas Petrakides being a man of honour, of integrity.

Of responsibility.

When she'd made her decision to find him, those descriptions had seemed like promises.

Now they were threats.

She didn't want Annabel to be someone's loveless responsibility. A burden. Yet now she realised she didn't have much choice.

She'd given her choices away when she'd embarked on this reckless mission.

'You will stay here until the issue of Annabel's paternity is resolved,' Lukas continued in implacable tones.

She'd expected as much, but his autocratic dictate still rankled. How about saying please? 'What about my responsibilities back home?' she demanded. 'My job, my life?'

'You can't spare a few days?' He raised one eyebrow in contemptuous disbelief. 'Surely you've already arranged a leave of absence?'

'Yes, but only for a few days…' She'd had holiday coming to her, as she rarely took days off.

'Then arrange some more.'

'It's not that simple…'

'Actually,' Lukas replied coolly, 'it is. Annabel is your first responsibility now—as you have told me yourself. You are her legal guardian aren't you? For the moment.'

For the moment. Panic fluttered through her insides, left her weak and afraid. 'Yes, I am. But I'm under no obligation…'

Lukas waved this empty threat aside with scathing contempt. 'Do not think to outmanoeuvre or outrank me, Miss Davies. I don't care what the law says. If Annabel is related to me, I will be the one deciding what place you may have in her life…if any. Is that understood?'

Rhiannon blinked in shock at the cold assessment. *If any?* 'I'm her guardian… You can't—'

'If you didn't want to start this,' Lukas informed her with soft menace, 'you shouldn't have come. No one would have been any the wiser.'

'I came,' Rhiannon replied jerkily, 'because it was my responsibility to find her true family—'

'So let me fulfil *my* responsibility,' Lukas interjected with cold finality. 'Until her future is decided, you will remain.'

And then she would be dismissed. The thought frightened her. It hurt, and she hadn't expected it to.

It wasn't supposed to be like this.

Rhiannon knew there was no point in arguing, no use in being angry. He had the power, the money, and the expensive legal team to enforce whatever he wished; she had nothing. She didn't even know what her rights were, hadn't even checked. After all, it wasn't supposed to have turned out like this.

'Fine. I'll stay…but on my terms. Annabel is still in my care, and nothing has been proved yet.'

'Indeed. In the meantime, you can move to a better room. A private suite.'

Rhiannon stared at him. It was a generous offer, but it was also a way to control her. Imprison her. 'I'm not moving rooms.'

'You must. You would be more comfortable, and so would the child. Besides, there is more privacy. Here—' he motioned to the expanse of beach '—anyone could come along. Photographers included.'

'Photographers?' Rhiannon repeated blankly, only to have him stare at her in disbelief.

'Paparazzi. Since you have so publicly announced that I have a child, the tabloid press are no doubt starting to swarm, clamouring for a photo or statement. I'd prefer for you—and the child—to be removed from such things.'

Rhiannon nodded jerkily, her mind whirling, becoming numb. 'All right.'

A cry pierced the stillness of the late afternoon, and Lukas jerked in surprise at the sound. Rhiannon hurried inside.

Annabel was sitting up in her cot, her hair matted sweatily to her flushed face, arms held up in helpless appeal.

Rhiannon scooped her up, breathed in her baby scent. It was becoming familiar, she realised. It was becoming dear.

Annabel's arms crept around her neck, held on. She nestled her chubby face in the curve of Rhiannon's shoulder and something in her splintered, fell apart to reveal the raw, aching need underneath.

She wanted this child.

She wanted to love her…and to be loved back.

She'd tried to hold the tide of emotions back, but they came anyway.

And now it looked as if Lukas Petrakides wasn't going to let that happen.

She turned, aware of his presence in the doorway. The fading sunlight outlined him in bronze, touching his hair with gold.

There was a look of fierce longing in his eyes, something deep and primal, before he noted tonelessly, 'She likes you.'

'We're starting to bond,' Rhiannon admitted cautiously. 'It's only been two weeks.'

'Two weeks? When did Leanne die?'

'Tuesday.'

Lukas stared at her in surprise, a frown marring the perfection of his features, putting a crease in his forehead. 'Four days ago?'

Rhiannon's hands stroked Annabel's back, her arms curling protectively around her warm little body. 'Yes. She only showed up on my doorstep a little over two weeks ago, and she died ten days later. Annabel has been in my sole care since then.'

'So there's been no time to formally adopt her?' Lukas surmised.

Rhiannon's arms tightened so that Annabel let out a squeal of protest.

'No, but Leanne did make me Annabel's legal guardian. I have the papers to prove it. It satisfied the immigration authorities, so it should be enough for you.' She lifted her chin. 'Annabel is *mine.*'

'If you wanted her to be,' Lukas said quietly. 'Somehow I don't think you do.'

Hurt and fury rippled through her at his brutal assessment. 'You're making assumptions,' she replied through gritted teeth. 'Annabel needs her bottle. So you'll have to excuse me.'

She turned away, escaped to the bathroom, where she'd rinsed out Annabel's army of bottles. She set the baby in her car seat and with shaking fingers measured out the powdered formula.

'Quite a set-up you've got here,' Lukas remarked, one shoulder propped against the doorway.

Rhiannon nearly dropped the bottle.

'Could I please have some privacy?'

'No. Annabel's now as much of my concern as she is yours. I don't plan on letting either of you out of my sight.'

Rhiannon's mouth twisted. 'Do you think I'll make a run for it?'

'I don't know what you're capable of,' Lukas admitted coolly. 'Or what you want. I wonder what you're after from this deal, Rhiannon Davies. Is Annabel your bargaining chip?'

She whirled around, the bottle flying out of her hand and landing on the tiled floor with a clatter. Annabel began to wail.

'I don't know what type of people you consort with,' she hissed furiously, 'but they must be different from the kind I'm used to. Because I would never, never stoop so low. I'm not in this for myself, Mr Petrakides. I'm here for Annabel, and all I care about is her wellbeing. If that means being without me, then I'll let her go. If it means being with me, then I'll fight tooth and nail to keep her. But I'm not going to obey your every barked-out command, or cater to your controlling whims. If I do anything—*anything*—it will be in consideration of Annabel only. Not you. Understood?'

She stood, chest heaving, fists clenched, and Lukas stared at her long and hard, his mouth tightening into a thin line of resolve before he gave a slight, self-mocking bow of acknowledgement.

'Understood.'

'Good.' She still didn't know if he believed her, but she didn't care. She was shaking, trembling from head to foot, as she scooped up Annabel, pressed her downy cheek against her pounding heart. Annabel, sensing her fear and anger, kept crying.

'You're in no state to hold her right now,' Lukas admonished, and he eased the baby from her reluctant grasp.

Rhiannon watched as he cradled her carefully, awkwardly. He wasn't used to babies, she thought.

The smile he gave Annabel was tender, his eyes widening in surprise at his own reaction to her toothless grin.

Rhiannon scooped the bottle from the floor and dumped it in the sink. As Annabel began to grizzle again, from hunger, she set to making another one.

She didn't know what was going to happen now, and she wasn't looking forward to finding out.

All she knew was the next few days might determine the rest of Annabel's life…and hers.

Several hours later Annabel was finally asleep. Stars glittered in an inky sky, reflected back in diamond pinpoints on the water, and Rhiannon prowled restlessly around the suite Lukas had insisted she move into a few hours ago. She'd never seen such luxury, and if the circumstances had been different she might have enjoyed it.

She ran a hand over the silky duvet on the king-sized bed, glanced in mocking derision at the whirlpool bath for two. All the trappings for romance, and totally unnecessary.

There was a separate sitting area, as well as a kitchenette filled with gleaming appliances and crockery—admittedly handy for dealing with Annabel's bottles and food.

A wide balcony stretched the entire length of the suite, and after one last check to make sure Annabel was settled Rhiannon slipped out into the warm cover of darkness.

She sank into a chair, brought her knees up to her chest and rested her chin on top. It was a pose from childhood—a pose of protection.

She closed her eyes.

She could hear the sounds of a party from the resort's gardens—was Lukas there? She hadn't seen him since he'd had her moved up here. Out of sight.

For the last few hours she'd entertained Annabel, fed and bathed her, keeping the doubts, the fears at bay.

Now they hurtled back with startling force.

Lukas had the power to take custody of Annabel, she realised dejectedly. She knew she was Annabel's legal guardian but the courts could easily decide in Lukas's favour—he had the support of extended family, including the baby's biological father. He was wealthy, powerful, connected to all the right people...

Anyway, this was what she'd wanted, she told herself. She'd come to France for Annabel to meet her father, to have a family.

The family she'd never had herself.

She'd *wanted* Lukas to take custody of Annabel, *to love her.* She'd convinced herself it was best for everyone.

She just hadn't expected it to hurt so much. She hadn't prepared herself for the surge of protectiveness she'd felt when Lukas had threatened paternity tests, custody suits.

She'd expected to offer Annabel, not to have her taken by force. Taken as a matter of duty rather than of love.

Duty. The word rested heavily on her. Lukas was a man of responsibility. He would do the right thing by Annabel, but he wouldn't love her.

Would he?

Not like I do. Not like I could.

She shook her head, dashed her hand against her eyes and the tears that threatened to fall. One fell anyway. This was stupid; she was being ridiculous. *She didn't cry.*

She had known this would happen—even if she hadn't anticipated the exact unfolding of events. She would just have to steel herself against the repercussions in her own heart.

'I thought you might be hungry.'

Rhiannon looked up in surprise. She'd been so lost in her own unhappy thoughts that she hadn't heard the glass door slide open, hadn't seen Lukas step out onto the balcony.

Yet now she felt him—felt the way his presence seemed to suck the air right from her lungs.

He was looking down at her with a quiet thoughtfulness that reminded her of that first moment in the bar.

Then she'd believed he was a kind man.

Now she wasn't sure.

Responsibility, integrity… They were good things, but they weren't kindness. They didn't encompass love.

She knew that well. Too well.

He placed a plate of food on the glass-topped table in front of her, then took her chin between his forefinger and thumb.

'You've been crying.'

'No, I haven't.'

In response his thumb traced the track of the tear down her cheek, straight to her heart.

'No?' he queried gently, and another tear followed silently, dripped onto his thumb.

Rhiannon jerked her chin out of his hand, scrubbed angrily at her eyes. 'I don't cry.'

He watched her thoughtfully for a moment. 'Why don't you eat? The lack of food won't help things.'

'Thank you,' Rhiannon mumbled, and self-consciously drew the plate towards her.

'A Languedoc speciality,' Lukas informed her as she dug into the beef stew. 'Made with black olives and garlic, finished with red wine.'

'Delicious,' Rhiannon admitted after one bite. She'd never had such food before.

He sat across from her, watching her with fathomless eyes. 'How long had it been since you'd seen this Leanne?' he asked after a long moment, and Rhiannon looked up in surprise.

'I hadn't seen her for ten years before she showed up on my doorstep with Annabel, asking me to take her.' She paused, toying with her fork, lost in memory.

'It must have been quite an inconvenience,' Lukas commented, his voice neutral. Yet Rhiannon still heard the judgement. Felt it.

'All children are inconveniences,' she said. 'That doesn't mean they're not worth it.'

'Doesn't it?' There was a cynical note to Lukas's tone that Rhiannon didn't like.

'What are you proposing to do?' she forced herself to ask. 'If Christos is the father? If Annabel is such an inconvenience to you...?'

'You think I'd palm her off like you've been trying to do?' Lukas finished, and Rhiannon jerked back at the scorn in his voice. 'I do my duty, Rhiannon. I'll do it by Annabel.'

'I was not palming her off,' she protested, and Lukas shrugged, unconvinced. Unimpressed.

'Call it what you like.'

'I was prepared to give you custody,' she admitted painfully, driven to the truth. 'A child should be with her natural-born parent—if that parent *wants* her.' She gazed unseeingly before her, the star-spangled sky blurring into a haze of colour. 'The parameters have changed now, though.'

'Yes, they have.' Lukas's voice was quiet, but held the underlying steel Rhiannon was coming to recognise...and dread. 'But some things remain the same.'

'Your nephew might not even be Annabel's father,' she pointed out.

'Perhaps he is not,' Lukas agreed implacably. 'But until the matter is resolved you will stay here. With me. When his paternity is proved—'

'*If*—'

'If,' he agreed smoothly. 'We will have matters to discuss.'

Rhiannon swallowed. She didn't want to ask what matters those might be—didn't have the courage. *I will decide what place you have in her life...if any.* She had a feeling, a terrible suspicion, that Lukas would cut her out of Annabel's life as if wielding a pair of scissors.

And she'd started it all by coming here. By looking for Lukas.

Had she anticipated what might happen when she found him?

Yes, she had. She'd pictured Lukas cradling his daughter, his face suffused with tenderness. She'd anticipated shock, followed by gratitude and joy.

She'd anticipated, she acknowledged numbly, a ridiculous happily-ever-after that was never going to happen.

It hadn't happened before. Why should it happen now?

She'd been a naive, foolish *idiot* to think for one moment that it could.

Lukas placed his hand on her own. His voice was a condemnation. 'This is what you wanted.'

'No, it isn't.'

'You came here to give her away,' Lukas continued flatly, and Rhiannon shrugged helplessly.

'To someone who would love her. I wanted...' She stared down at their hands, his large brown one on top of her paler, more delicate fingers. 'I wanted her to have a family.'

Lukas was silent, his fingers heavy on hers. She felt his warmth, his heat, and it fanned quickly, alarmingly, into a more dangerous flame.

Desire.

Suddenly it was there, thrumming to life, palpable, heady, filled with possibility.

She wanted to jerk her hand away, but Lukas's hand was still on hers, still heavy, staying her own movements. And somehow Rhiannon knew she wouldn't move her hand even if it were free.

She watched as he turned her hand over, traced his thumb lightly down her palm. Rhiannon shivered. She was helplessly in thrall to him, to the barest of his touches.

She snuck a look at him from beneath her lowered lashes, saw he was staring at their hands too, watching his own thumb flick along her palm with an almost clinical interest, as if he too were captive to a greater need than either one of them had ever anticipated or experienced.

Then his eyes met hers, and Rhiannon was rocked to her core by the blatant need, the open hunger in them.

He reached out his other hand, slowly, deliberately, and tangled it in her hair. Rhiannon's mouth opened soundlessly, yet she didn't resist as he pulled her towards him, nearly out of her chair. He leaned forward, his lips a breath away from hers.

'I want to do this.' He spoke in a ragged whisper; it was a confession.

Rhiannon's head swum dizzily. *So do I.* Yet she couldn't quite say it.

Lukas must have sensed her unspoken permission, or perhaps he didn't require it, for he touched his lips to hers once—a brush, a flicker, a promise.

Then the promise deepened into a certainty as his tongue plundered her mouth, took possession of her soul. Rhiannon's fingers bunched on his shoulders, clawed for purchase, for sanity.

Somehow she had slipped out of her chair, was kneeling on the hard tiled floor between Lukas's powerful thighs. She could feel his arousal against her heart.

His mouth continued to cover hers, plunging, plundering. Taking everything. His hands fisted in her hair, drawing her closer, binding her to him.

The kiss went on endlessly. She'd never felt so treasured, so desired, so needed.

So loved.

The thought was a cold slap of reality, a mocking laugh in the stillness of their entwined bodies.

There was no love involved here. She barely knew this man. All he felt for her was contempt, suspicion. She wanted him—oh, yes—and he wanted her.

But that was all.

Sex.

She pulled away, wincing as her hair tangled around Lukas's fingers. He was completely still, his hand still snarled in her hair, staring at her as if she were a stranger—as if he were a stranger to himself.

His breathing was ragged, uneven, and so was hers.

'I'm sorry.' He looked appalled, angry. Yet Rhiannon had a feeling that anger was not directed at her. Carefully he unwound the strands of hair from his fingers, smoothed the curls back from her fevered brow. 'That shouldn't have happened.'

'No,' Rhiannon agreed shakily, although the sense of loss she felt would have sent her to her knees if she hadn't already been there.

Lukas helped her back into her chair. 'Clearly I've been without a woman for too long,' he said with a cool smile, and Rhiannon's own mouth twisted in bitterness.

'That's what that was about? Sex?' Of course it was. She was such a pathetic fool, thinking for one second it could ever be anything more.

Lukas sat back, looking surprised. 'Obviously I desire you. I desired you when I first saw you.'

'In the bar.'

He looked discomfited for the barest of moments before he gave a quick, sharp nod. 'Yes. Before any of this happened with the child the desire was there. It was real.'

Real and warm and alive. Yet it was just desire—cheap and easy. Even desire could be a burden.

It wasn't love, and Rhiannon knew that was what she needed. Wanted.

She'd just never had it.

'We should go to bed. Sleep,' she amended hastily, and Lukas acknowledged her slip of the tongue with a wry nod. 'It's been a long day.'

'Yes, it has.'

Rhiannon reached for her plate and he stilled her movement with one hand on her arm, his fingers curling around her wrist. 'Perhaps that was a moment of comfort we both needed,' he said. 'It won't happen again.'

He spoke in warning, as if he thought she might expect a replay. Did she seem so desperate?

Rhiannon's nerves were splintered, her emotions in tatters.

None of this was supposed to happen.

'Well, thank you,' she finally said, her voice strained and low, 'for that courtesy.' And without another word, not trusting herself to speak or meet his frowning gaze, she slipped through the door.

She heard him leave the suite from the safety of the locked bathroom. She sat on the edge of the bathtub, her fists in her hair, her lips still burning from his kisses.

Perhaps it was a moment of comfort we both needed.

Damned by compassion. Pity. No doubt his misguided sense of responsibility striking once again. He'd been trying to comfort her.

She didn't want comfort.

She wanted love.

She wanted it for herself, wanted it for Annabel.

She felt a terrible, hollow certainty that she wouldn't find it here.

CHAPTER FOUR

'WE NEED to leave. Now.'

Rhiannon sat up in bed, blinking sleep from her eyes, clutching the covers to her chest. Annabel was still asleep, and Lukas stood in the doorway of her suite, fully dressed, his lithe body coiled and tense.

'What are you talking about?'

'What I'm talking about,' he bit out, 'is the press in front of this resort—thanks to the little stunt you pulled yesterday at the reception.' He pulled a rolled-up newspaper from his pocket and threw it on the bed.

Rhiannon unfurled it with shaking fingers and a leaden heart. *Secret Playboy? Lukas Petrakides Discovers his Love-child. Furious Mother Booted Out of Newest Resort!* the headline screamed. There was even a picture—a grainy shot from a telephoto lens—of the two of them on the beach. The paparazzi photographer had clearly waited for his moment, Rhiannon realised with a sinking feeling. It was towards the end of their conversation yesterday afternoon, when they had clearly been in an argument.

Thank God they hadn't got a photo of their kiss last night. Just the memory caused a flush to crawl up her throat.

She looked up, met Lukas's blazing eyes. 'I'm sorry.'

'We can discuss this later,' he informed her tersely. 'Right now we need to leave. I have a private jet departing in twenty minutes for Greece. You and Annabel will be on it.'

'Greece?' Rhiannon repeated stupidly, and he slashed a hand through the air.

'Yes—to safety! You can't stay here now the press have wind of this story. Once they know we've gone, they'll give up the chase. For the moment. I don't want the press hounding the resort's guests, and I don't want them finding you or Annabel. The last thing I need is more sordid details.'

That was what she was, Rhiannon thought. A sordid detail. She opened her mouth to reply, but Lukas cut her off before she could frame a syllable.

'Get dressed. I'll wait outside the door.'

He flung open the door just as Annabel let out her good-morning howl of hunger.

Rhiannon scooped her up, prepared a bottle with clumsy fingers and a whirling mind. She dressed herself quickly, then found something for Annabel to wear, threw some nappies and the prepared bottle in a bag, and stepped outside.

'I'm ready.'

'Good.' Lukas had been leaning against the wall, arms folded, but now he pushed off and stood back to sweep her with an assessing gaze.

Rhiannon was conscious of her faded jeans and worn tee-shirt. Annabel had already dribbled on her shoulder. Lukas's mouth tightened as he looked at her, whether in disapproval or displeasure Rhiannon didn't know, but she forced herself not to care.

'Someone will bring your bags to the jet. Let's go,' he said, and as he strode quickly down the corridor she had no choice but to follow, Annabel screeching in protest.

Lukas sat back in the plane seat and rolled his shoulders, trying to relieve the stabbing tension which had lodged there since he'd seen those damn newspapers this morning.

He knew the news would be all over France, all over Greece, all over the world. His father would have seen it this morning. He would be furious.

Lukas had failed him, failed the family, by allowing such lies to be smeared across papers and television screens.

Yet Lukas dismissed the thought of his father in contemplation of the woman shrouded in misery opposite him. Rhiannon sat with Annabel on her lap, her face averted towards the window.

Lukas felt an unwelcome twinge of unease. He no longer believed Rhiannon was a blackmailer, yet he still didn't trust her. He *couldn't* trust a woman who was willing to give up a child entrusted into her care, no matter what excuse she gave…or what she had convinced herself to believe.

He suspected she'd persuaded herself it was for the best, that she was acting nobly, yet he saw the truth in her hunched position, in the awkward way she held the baby.

She wasn't used to children, he thought. She probably lived in a chic little flat that wasn't equipped for infants. No doubt she was eager to get back to her life…her lover. The thought made his expression harden in distaste…and in remembrance.

It doesn't matter to me. Take him.

He shook his head, banishing the memory, the mocking voice.

This was a different situation, a different woman…even if some aspects seemed the same.

His thoughts shifted to the baby in Rhiannon's arms. Her dark, curly hair and soulful eyes reminded him of photographs of himself as a baby. She had the look of a Petrakides. If Annabel was indeed Christos's daughter, which to Lukas now seemed a near certainty, there could be no question of her future. It would be in Greece, with the Petrakides family.

And, he acknowledged with grim certainty, Rhiannon Davies would not fit into that picture at all.

The baby gave a little shuddering sigh, and Rhiannon stroked her downy hair, a tender smile lighting her face. Lukas watched, feeling a now-familiar tightening in his gut. In his heart.

She looked as if she cared for the child, but he couldn't believe it. Didn't want to. It would be much easier for everyone, he mused, if there was no emotional attachment between Rhiannon and Annabel. Still, even if there were, he was confident he could convince her to return to Wales, to relinquish through the courts her guardianship of the child. All it took was the right price.

He watched Rhiannon smooth an errant curl back from her forehead, and he was suddenly stabbingly reminded of his own hand in those tangled curls, drawing her to him, tasting her wine-sweetened lips, burrowing himself in the warmth of her.

The kiss last night had been a mistake. A mind-blowing, sense-scattering event, but an error nonetheless. He'd wanted her; he still did. He didn't completely understand his desire for such a slight, average-looking woman, but he acknowledged the truth of it. Perhaps he had been without a woman for too long; perhaps it was something more.

It didn't matter. He never gave in to desire, never catered to need.

What mattered was his family, the Petrakides name, and his duty towards it. That was all.

Two hours later the jet landed on the airstrip of the Petrakides private island.

Rhiannon stared numbly out of the window at the sparkling blue-green of the Aegean Sea, at the rocky shore leading up to landscaped gardens and a long, low, rambling villa of white-washed stone.

'Come,' Lukas said, taking her hand as he helped her out of the plane. 'My father will be waiting.'

Rhiannon transferred a sleeping Annabel to her other shoulder as she stepped out into the sunshine. The air was hot and dry, the sky a hard, bright blue.

She inhaled the dry, dusty scent of rosemary and olive trees, combined with the salty tang of the sea. Annabel stirred, rubbed her eyes with her fists, and then looked around in sleepy wonder.

'Wait here.' Lukas stayed her with one firm hand, his countenance darkening with suppressed tension by the second.

A man was striding stiffly towards them. Tall, spare and white haired. Rhiannon had no doubt this was Theo Petrakides, founder of the Petrakides real estate empire. And he looked furious.

She stepped backwards into the shadow of the plane as the two men squared off.

Theo said something in rapid Greek; Lukas replied. A muscle bunched in his jaw but his voice was flat and calm, his posture almost relaxed.

This was a man in control. A man who did not give in to emotions, whims. Desires.

What about last night? Rhiannon shook her head in denial of the question her heart asked but her mind wouldn't answer.

Last night had been a moment of weakness for both of them and, as Lukas had said, it wouldn't happen again.

They were still speaking in rapid but controlled tones. Then Annabel let out a squeal as a gull soared low overhead, and Theo Petrakides's sharp grey gaze swung to her.

Rhiannon froze, her arms tight around a now struggling Annabel. Her heart rate was erratic and fast as the older man walked slowly towards her. He stood in front of her, a flat look in his eyes.

'This is the child? Christos's child?' he said slowly in English.

'We don't know yet for certain,' Rhiannon managed carefully, her voice a cracked whisper.

'His bastard.'

She jerked back as if slapped, saw the frank condemnation in Theo's eyes. She glanced involuntarily at Lukas, saw him shake his head in silent warning. Still, fury bubbled up within her, gave her courage.

'Annabel Weston is in my care,' she told the man quietly. 'She is my responsibility, no matter who the father turns out to be.'

He glanced at her, reluctant admiration flickering briefly in his eyes before he shrugged. 'We shall see.'

Panic rose in her throat, and she tasted bile. Was Theo implying that they would take Annabel away from her if Christos was the father? Lukas had said something similar.

Why had she not considered how this might happen?

Because you wanted the fairy tale.

Theo strode away, and Lukas put his arm around Rhiannon's shoulders, guiding her towards the rocky path that led to the villa.

'None of you want her,' she choked out in a whisper, and Lukas simply shrugged.

'It's not a question of want.'

'But of responsibility, right?' She shook her head. 'I wanted more for Annabel.'

'I'm afraid,' Lukas said quietly, 'that what you want is not my primary consideration.'

She glanced at him, saw the grim determination hardening his eyes, his mouth, his words, and felt a stab of fear. She was not his primary consideration…or any consideration at all, she finished bleakly.

An hour later Rhiannon prowled restlessly around her bedroom. It was large and spacious, with a wide balcony overlooking the sea. Annabel sat on the floor, playing happily with some seashells Rhiannon had found in a decorative bowl.

There was a light knock on the door, and with her heart rising straight into her throat she called out, 'Come in.'

Lukas opened the door. He'd changed from his business attire, was now dressed in jeans and a white cotton shirt open at the throat. Those few undone buttons revealed a tanned column of skin that Rhiannon couldn't seem to tear her gaze from.

'Have you found everything to your satisfaction?' he asked, and she jerked her eyes upwards towards his face.

His hair was damp, brushed back from his face, his eyes sparkling silver as he smiled with a wry amusement that caused her face to burn with humiliated realisation.

He knew how he affected her, and he thought it was amusing. No doubt he had women falling for him all the time, and he obviously had no problem putting them in their place. Rejecting them.

'Yes, fine,' she said shortly.

He glanced at her still unopened suitcase by the bed. 'You haven't unpacked.'

'We're not going to be here for long.'

'Perhaps not,' Lukas agreed. 'But it would be more comfortable, certainly, to enjoy a short stay.'

'Before I'm booted out?' Rhiannon interjected. 'Sorry, I don't feel like complying.'

Lukas shrugged, ran a hand through his hair. Rhiannon watched as it flopped boyishly across his forehead; she resisted the urge to brush it back with itching fingers.

'Suit yourself,' he said. 'I only thought you might want to be comfortable.'

'I don't want to be comfortable,' she snapped, even though she knew she was being childish.

Lukas's eyes flashed. 'You should—at least for Annabel's sake. Surely it is in her best interests for both of you to be relaxed and comfortable during your stay here? It is, in fact, your responsibility,' he continued in a harder voice, 'to be so.'

Rhiannon's mouth pursed in annoyance. 'It's all about responsibility, isn't it?'

For a half-second Lukas looked nonplussed. 'Of course it is.'

'Not love.'

His eyebrows rose. 'Who am I supposed to love?'

'Annabel!' Rhiannon cried, too angry and despairing to be embarrassed that he might have actually thought she meant *herself*. 'I came here so she could find her father…a father who would love her!'

'But I am not her father,' he reminded her. 'And I cannot love a child I've never even seen before. Not right away.'

'Especially one that is not yours, I suppose?' Rhiannon finished, and he shook his head, dismissing her jibe.

'If Annabel is Christos's child—which I believe she is—then I will make sure she is cared for. Absolutely.'

Rhiannon's mouth dried. *Absolutely.* It was a word that didn't allow for difficulties, differences. Flexibility. It was a cold, hard, unyielding word, and she didn't like it. 'I didn't want it to be like this,' she finally said after a moment, her eyes averted.

'I understand. But this is now how it is. How it will be remains for me to decide.'

'You,' Rhiannon said, 'and not me, I suppose?'

Lukas shook his head. 'I don't know what you want from me.

If you came to the Petra resort to find Annabel's father, you suc-
ceeded. You did your duty. Now you will leave the rest to us.'

'I'm not going to leave it up to you,' Rhiannon protested.
'Annabel is my ward, not yours. Any decisions that are made will
involve me.' Her voice came out more strident than she intended,
and Annabel looked up anxiously. Rhiannon bent down, soothed
her with a few hushing motions.

'The only decision that has been made so far,' Lukas said,
with a deliberate patience that warned Rhiannon he was close
to losing his temper, 'is for you to remain here until the
question of paternity is resolved. All I'm asking now is that
you stay here, in comfort, not snapping and biting like a fish
on a line, and enjoy a few days in what most people consider
to be paradise.'

Rhiannon watched Annabel bang two shells together, her eyes
wide and round. Lukas's analogy was dead on, she realised
grimly. She did feel like a fish on a line, dangling desperately—
and, worse yet, she'd willingly put the hook in her own mouth.

'A few days—and then what?'

'That remains to be seen.' His mouth was a thin line, his eyes
dangerously blank, and Rhiannon knew better than to press him
now. She wasn't going to ask questions she didn't want answers to.

'Fine,' she said heavily. 'Have you spoken to Christos?'

'No. He is on a friend's yacht at the moment. I've left a
message on his mobile, but he probably won't answer it until he
is on shore.' His mouth twisted, tightened in derision. 'He doesn't
like his holidays disturbed.'

'And this is the man you want for Annabel's father?' Rhiannon
said with a shake of her head.

'No, this is the man who *is* Annabel's father. We cannot
change that…if it is proved.'

He glanced down at the baby, frowning as he saw her suck
the edge of a shell. 'Do you think this is an appropriate toy for
the child?' he asked, taking the offending item from a reluctant
Annabel, who immediately howled in outrage.

Rhiannon scooped her up, pressed the baby to her body in a

defensive gesture. 'It's the best I could do. Leanne had few toys for Annabel, and there hasn't been time…'

'I will make sure that you are both adequately supplied while you're here,' Lukas said, although there was still a frowning furrow on his forehead.

'We don't need anything from you,' Rhiannon protested, as Annabel began to tug rather painfully on her earring.

The look Lukas gave her was swift, searching. Knowing. 'On the contrary,' he corrected quietly, 'there are many things you need from me. That is why you came, is it not?'

Before she could answer, he sketched a brief bow of farewell and left her alone.

'Ouch!' Rhiannon disengaged Annabel's chubby fingers from her earring. 'Not so hard, sweetheart.' She set the baby back on the floor, prowled the room once more.

Her heart was racing in time with her thoughts, whirling helplessly, out of reach, out of answers.

After a moment she flung open the doors to the balcony, went outside and breathed in the clean sea air. She needed it to steady her, for her senses were still reeling from Lukas's presence, his power.

He seemed determined to take responsibility for Annabel. To care for her.

This was what she had wanted—yet not like this. Never like this. With Annabel as discarded goods, unwanted, thrust on someone who believed he needed to do his duty.

Her life would be loveless; she would grow up with the cold knowledge that she'd only been taken in because there had been no other place for her, because no one had wanted her.

As Rhiannon had grown up.

I want her. The words burned in her brain and lit her soul. *I want her.* She would not give Annabel up so easily. When she'd envisaged giving her up, it had been to a loving home, to a father who wanted her. Who loved her.

A fantasy, she acknowledged now, and perhaps she realised that from the moment she'd spoken to Lukas Petrakides. A fantasy based on what she'd always wanted—always dreamed of—for herself.

But this was not about her, or her lost dreams. It was about Annabel. And she would not condemn the infant to a childhood like she'd had. She'd come to France, to Lukas, to keep that from happening. Now that things had changed she would do what was necessary to keep Annabel from being the burden she herself had been.

She'd thought that meant walking away. Now it meant staying.

'The girl must go.'

Lukas jerked his contemplative gaze away from the study window and turned to see his father standing still and erect in the doorway. Though his hair was snow white, his face lined, Theo Petrakides was still a handsome and imposing man.

He was also dying.

The doctors had told Lukas that Theo had a few good months left in him—but it would go downhill from there. Theo knew; he accepted it with the grim stoicism with which he'd accepted all the tragedies in his life.

'I'll die well,' he'd said with cold detachment. 'I'll do my duty.'

Yes, Lukas knew Theo would do his duty in death—as he had in life.

Just as he would do his. His promise to care for Annabel had not been rash. As soon as the possibility had arisen that Christos might be the father Lukas had known what it would mean. The sacrifice he would have to make.

Caring for a child, he told himself, was hardly difficult. He'd hire a nanny, enlist the best help. It might mean travelling a bit less to be more available to her as a father. That thought, that *word,* shook him more than he cared to admit.

Still, he would do what needed to be done to provide for the child and, more importantly, to keep the Petrakides name free from scandal or shame. He would do his duty.

'What girl?' he asked now, forcing his mind back to the present, to the frowning countenance of his father.

'That English girl. She has no place in our lives, Lukas.'

Lukas's palm curled into a fist on the smooth, mahogany-topped desk. Slowly, deliberately, he flattened it out again. 'She's Welsh, and her name is Rhiannon. She does have a place in our lives, Papa—she's Annabel's guardian.'

Theo's eyebrows rose at hearing the casual, almost intimate way Lukas referred to both Rhiannon and Annabel.

Lukas realised he'd spoken about Rhiannon as if he knew her, liked her. He shrugged. What he said was still true.

'For now,' the older man agreed flatly. 'But when Christos—damn him!—is shown to be the father, she will have no place at all. You told me she's not related, just a friend of the mother. We are blood relations, and we will do our duty—even for Christos's English bastard.'

'Is that what you plan on telling the child, when she is old enough to hear?'

'I won't be around then,' Theo replied with brutal frankness, 'so you can do the honours. She can hardly complain if she has been well provided for. No one can accuse us of being ungenerous.'

'No, indeed,' Lukas agreed dryly, and Theo frowned.

'Don't tell me you've a fondness for that English piece?'

'She's *Welsh,* and, no, I have not. But I prefer to speak about any woman with respect.'

'She will only complicate matters,' Theo continued, ignoring his son. He strode to the window, watched the waves crash onto the rocky shore. 'If she isn't already attached to the child, she will become so, and we cannot have the bad press of a messy custody case. The tabloids would make a meal of this, Lukas. You've already seen what they've done with these rumours of your mistress and your love-child.'

'I have,' he replied tightly. 'But I believe Rhiannon is willing to be reasonable if we approach her with sensitivity. I don't want to take her from the child now. Annabel has had a great deal of upheaval in her life, and it would do none of us any favours to send Rhiannon away before she is settled.'

Theo glanced shrewdly at his son. 'None of us?' he repeated, and gave a dry chuckle. 'Oh, very well. If you must have her, have her. You've been without a woman too long, haven't you? You never learned how to be discreet in such matters.'

'I prefer to be restrained.' Lukas's head was throbbing with fury. He knew he should be used to his father's frank, crass ways—and he knew his father believed duty was a public matter, rather than a private one. As long as people saw what you did was right, it hardly mattered what you thought.

He felt differently.

'This would be solved,' Theo continued in a harder voice, 'if you did your duty to provide me with an heir and marry.'

'You know I never plan to marry.'

'Your duty—'

'I refuse to marry a woman I love,' Lukas intervened flatly, 'and I refuse to marry without love. It would not be fair to the woman.'

'There are plenty of women who would marry without love,' Theo scoffed.

Lukas suppressed a sigh. They'd had this conversation many times.

'Scheming gold-diggers or materialistic snobs,' he dismissed. 'Hardly suitable material.' The thought of not providing an heir for the Petrakides empire was an uncomfortable one, but he knew his limits. Marriage was outside of them. As was love.

'Fine,' Theo said, willing to let go of this thorny subject for a moment. 'Still, the English bit goes.' He stared his son down. 'And soon.'

Lukas gazed at his father. 'There is no question that she will leave when the child's paternity is determined,' he agreed coolly. 'There can be no place for her in our lives. But until then it would benefit us all to keep her sweet.' He busied himself with some papers on his desk. 'Now, I have work to do, Papa. I will see you at dinner.'

Theo glanced sharply at his son, but with a jerky nod he left the room.

Lukas swivelled to stare out of the window. The aquamarine sea stretched flatly to an endless horizon—yet he knew that only a few miles out there would be boats. Boats disguised as fishing vessels, but filled with photographers and journalists clamouring for an exclusive shot of Lukas with his illicit family. Photographs which would then be sold to tabloids around the world, to make the Petrakides name raked through the mud and the dirt once again.

He sighed, thrusting a hand through his hair. He understood the need to avoid bad press—God knew, the Petrakides family had had enough of it.

He also understood that Rhiannon Davies would have to go. As his father had said, her presence could only complicate matters, and he didn't want a Petrakides child—*any* child—attached to a woman whose motives in staying were at best uncertain, at worst suspect.

What did she want? he wondered, not for the first time. She didn't want to leave the child; she didn't want to stay. Lukas still wasn't sure if she was playing a high-stakes game, or if she simply didn't *know* what she wanted.

Hardly a woman to trust with a child, he thought in derisive dismissal. With a child's love.

Still, he had use of her, as did the child. He wasn't ready to release her just yet.

That night for dinner Rhiannon dressed in the outfit she'd worn yesterday to the reception—now slightly crumpled, but still clean at least.

She'd fed Annabel in the kitchen, under the eye of Adeia, the kindly housekeeper and cook. After giving the baby a bath in the huge tub in her adjoining bathroom, she'd put Annabel to sleep in the middle of the wide bed in her room. There were no travel cots, but Lukas had assured her one would be found by the next day.

Dinner, she'd been informed, was in the villa's dining room, and she was expected there at half past seven.

Rhiannon drew in a shaky breath and examined her reflection. Her hair had turned wild and curly due to the moisture in the sea air, and no amount of brushing or spray would tame it. She'd abandoned any pretence at styling it, and settled for a slick of lipstick, a dab of perfume, and her old outfit.

It wasn't as if she were trying to impress either Theo or Lukas. Though she dreaded seeing the older man again. His words rang in her ears.

Bastard.

That was all he saw Annabel as. What would he think, she wondered with wry bitterness, if he knew *she* was illegitimate too?

What would Lukas think? Would he judge her an unfit mother? Damn her for the circumstances of her birth, as Theo seemed willing to do?

Rhiannon threw back her shoulders, her mouth hardening into a grim line. That wasn't going to happen. Because she was going to stick around. No matter what they said. No matter what they did.

After checking that Annabel was deeply asleep—exhausted, no doubt, by the upheavals of the day—Rhiannon headed downstairs. The wide, sweeping staircase led to a tiled foyer flanked with mahogany double doors that led to the villa's reception rooms.

Lukas came into the foyer from one of the rooms at the sound of her heels clicking on the tiles. He wore a light grey button-down shirt, expensive and well made, and charcoal trousers cinched with a leather belt. He looked comfortable, walking with the innate arrogant grace of someone who was used to being watched, admired, obeyed.

He swept her with a cool gaze that made Rhiannon uncomfortably aware of her unruly hair, her crumpled outfit. Her position weak, helpless.

Hopeless.

Who was she kidding? She might put on a face of bravado, but that was all it was. False courage. If Lukas didn't want her here, there was nothing she could do to convince him to let her stay.

She swallowed, realising afresh how out of her depth she truly was.

Out of her mind.

Lukas said nothing, merely took her arm to lead her into the dining room.

The table was set, and Theo stood by the wide windows that overlooked the shoreline. The stars were just visible in a lavender sky, and a few lights twinkled on the water.

'Are there boats out there?' Rhiannon asked, moving closer to the window to look.

'Journalists,' Theo replied flatly. 'Hoping to get a good photo. They know if they come too close we can prosecute.' He spoke slowly, deliberately, as if she were stupid. Rhiannon bit her lip, bit down the annoyance at the man's condescension, and turned to Lukas.

'Have they followed you out here already?'

'They've followed you,' Theo interjected. He smiled, but his eyes were hard. 'Something to do with what you said, I should think. My son's baby.'

Rhiannon flushed at the condemnation in his tone. 'I'm sorry. I was desperate, and I didn't realise the tabloids would make such a fuss.'

Theo looked unconvinced. 'Didn't you? Haven't you read the papers before? The Petrakides family has, alas, been mentioned many times before.'

'Have they?' Rhiannon lifted her chin, her eyes shooting amber sparks. 'I do not read those kinds of papers, Mr Petrakides.'

Theo's mouth hardened, and he jerked a shoulder towards the table. 'Shall we?'

He was gentleman enough to wait to sit until she was seated, but Rhiannon didn't like the way he so quickly and coldly assessed her. Dismissed her. Lukas, she feared, felt the same way. He was simply better at hiding his feelings.

It didn't matter anyway. She couldn't let it matter.

Adeia brought in the first course—vine leaves stuffed with rice and herbs, and a separate dish of olives and feta marinated in olive oil.

It looked excellent, and with an audible growl of her stomach Rhiannon realised how hungry she was.

The first course was followed by moussaka, and a rack of lamb with herbs and served with rice.

It was delicious, and by the time dessert arrived—a nut cake flavoured with cloves and cinnamon—she was so full she felt the waistband of her skirt pinch uncomfortably.

She was also aware of Theo's disapproval of his son. He never said anything outright; in fact he spoke slowly, as if he wanted to use as few words as possible, and even chose those with care.

Still, she saw the disapproval in the tightening of his mouth, the flatness in his eyes, the biting edge of his tone.

Lukas, to his credit, remained mild and relaxed throughout the whole meal, although Rhiannon noticed how his eyes darkened, blanked. His fist bunched on the tablecloth before he forced himself to shrug, nod, smile. Dismiss.

She wondered at the tension in the relationship, what secrets the Petrakides family harboured. What secrets Lukas hid behind the neutral expression, the cold eyes.

This was Annabel's family. Fear and uncertainty churned in Rhiannon's stomach as she thought of giving up her ward to these people.

She couldn't. And she didn't have to, she reminded herself. Not yet. Maybe never.

After cups of strong Greek coffee, Theo jerkily excused himself to bed. He walked stiffly from the room, leaving Rhiannon and Lukas alone amidst the flickering candles and the remnants of a fantastic meal.

'That was wonderful…thank you.' She dabbed at her lips with her napkin, suddenly aware of a palpable tension.

Lukas was rotating his coffee cup slowly between strong, brown fingers, his expression shuttered.

He looked up when she spoke, smiled easily, the darkness of his eyes clearing like the sun coming from behind storm clouds. 'You're not going to end the evening so soon?'

'It's late… I'm tired…' She should be tired, but right now her senses were humming in a way that made her feel gloriously awake and alive. She knew to stay, to linger in the dim, intimate atmosphere of the room, would be dangerous for both of them.

For some reason this attraction had sprung up between

them—a powerful force that they both had to avoid…for Annabel's sake.

And for her own.

'Will you walk with me on the beach?' Lukas asked. 'There need not be enmity between us, Rhiannon.'

'Is that so?' Rhiannon tried to laugh; it came out brittle. 'It's easy for you to say that, Lukas. You're holding all the cards.'

'I think,' Lukas said carefully, 'we both want what's best for Annabel.'

'We might disagree about what that is.'

He nodded in acknowledgement, then shrugged. 'It's a beautiful moonlit night. The photographers can't see us in the dark. A few moments… You haven't had any fresh air since you've been here, and the island is beautiful.'

'I can't leave Annabel. If she wakes…'

'Adeia will listen for her,' Lukas said. 'She'd love to.'

Rhiannon hesitated. Perhaps getting to know Lukas would help. It might soften him to her case, to her hopes for Annabel. 'All right,' she agreed, not nearly as reluctantly as she knew she should. 'A few moments.'

Outside the sound of the surf was a muted roar in the distance, and the air was cool and soft. Lukas led her down a paved path to the beach, a stretch of smooth sand that curved around tumbled rocks into the unknown.

He kicked off his shoes, and Rhiannon did the same, enjoying the silky softness between her toes.

They walked quietly down the shoreline for a few minutes, the only sound the lapping of waves.

'Has this island been in your family long?' she finally asked, unnerved by the silence that had stretched between them.

Lukas gave a short, abrupt laugh before shaking his head. 'No, indeed not. Only about twenty-five years or so; the Petrakides fortune is very new.'

'Is it?' Rhiannon had not read that in the papers, but then she'd only been looking for salient details regarding the man she'd believed to be Annabel's father. 'I didn't realise.'

'My father started life as a street-sweeper,' Lukas stated with matter-of-fact flatness. 'He worked his way up to becoming landlord of a tenement in Athens, before banding together with a few partners and buying a block of derelict apartment buildings. They renovated them, turned them into modest, affordable housing units. And he moved up from there. Eventually he didn't need partners.'

'A real success story,' Rhiannon murmured, and Lukas acknowledged this with a brusque nod.

'Yes.'

They walked quietly for a moment, Lukas seeming lost in unhappy thoughts.

Success wasn't everything, Rhiannon supposed. It couldn't buy happiness. It couldn't buy love.

'Your father doesn't seem like a happy man,' she ventured, surprised by her own candour as well as by Lukas's swift, acknowledging glance.

'No, he isn't,' he agreed after a pause. 'If he seems in a bad temper, it is in part because he is upset over the press. My father has wanted to prove to everyone that he deserves the wealth and success he has earned. He feels any stain on his reputation is a reflection of where he came from—the street. Although...' Lukas's face was obscured in shadow, but there was suddenly a different darkness to his tone. 'Things have not been easy for him lately.'

Rhiannon's steps slowed as memories clicked into place. 'He's dying, isn't he?' she said quietly.

He stiffened, turned in surprise. 'How did you know?'

'I should have realised sooner,' she admitted. 'I'm a palliative nurse—I work in hospices. I've been around a lot of people in his situation.' She shook her head. 'I assumed he was speaking so slowly because he thought I was stupid, but it's because he's losing his words, isn't he? What does he have? A brain tumour?'

Lukas nodded stiffly. 'The doctors have given him at most a few more months. It hasn't, by the grace of God, affected him too much yet, although he occasionally forgets things. Sometimes it is just a word, other times a whole event.' He shook his head. 'It is frustrating, because he knows he is forgetting.'

'I'm sorry,' Rhiannon whispered. 'I know how difficult a dying parent can be.'

'Do you?' Lukas's glance was swift, sharp, assessing, yet there was a flicker of compassion in those silver eyes. 'Tell me about yourself, Rhiannon.'

She shrugged, discomfited by the turn in the conversation he'd so quickly and effortlessly made. 'My parents died three years ago,' she said, as if it were of no consequence. 'I cared for them until their deaths. It is a difficult thing to do.'

'Yes…I suppose it is. And in the time since then?'

'I studied nursing, went into hospice care. It made the most sense after my experience with my parents.'

'A rather lonely-sounding life,' Lukas remarked, his tone expressionless, his face in shadow.

'No more than anyone else's.' Irritation prickled at his judgement. 'I like to think I make a difference. Help people in a time of need that most of us would prefer to ignore.'

'Indeed, that's too true. I only meant that spending time with people twice your age no doubt makes it difficult to find friends with whom you can socialise.'

Rhiannon shrugged. She could hardly argue with that. She didn't *have* a social life—had never had one. She gazed unseeingly at the dark stretch of water, at the stars strung above in an inky sky like diamonds pricked through cloth.

'Why did you come here, Rhiannon?' Lukas asked after a long moment, his voice musing. 'Most women in your position I believe would not have made such an effort. They would have sent a letter, or gone through a solicitor. But to come to the resort, to the reception, and think you could convince me I was a child's father—!' He shook his head, smiling slightly in disbelief, but Rhiannon was only conscious of her own prickling, humiliated response.

'I admit it was foolhardy,' she said in a tight voice that bordered on strangled. She was glad the darkness hid her flushed face. 'I thought a face-to-face confrontation would be the…strongest way to present Annabel to you.'

'To get rid of her, you mean?'

'You have a strange way of looking at things,' she retorted. She stopped to turn and face him. 'I wanted to give her to her father—her family. I would have been ignoring my responsibility if I hadn't attempted to find you. Wouldn't I? To keep her to myself, to make no effort to find a family who might want her, love her…' She trailed off, shaking her head. 'That would have been selfish.'

Lukas was silent for a moment. 'You wanted to keep her?' he asked in a different voice.

'Of course I did—do! She's a baby.'

'An inconvenience, as you said.'

She glanced sharply at him, unsure if he thought that, or if he simply thought *she* did. 'All children are inconveniences,' she said flatly. 'If you remember, I said that didn't mean they weren't worth it.'

'So you want her, but you're prepared to give her up?' Lukas said musingly.

'I *was,*' Rhiannon emphasised. 'Now things are different.' She turned to face him. 'You should know that I won't give Annabel up now. I may have been willing to earlier, when I believed you were the father, when I thought you would love her. But I realise now the situation is completely different. I don't know how I can fit into the family you envisage for her—your family—but I *will* have some part. I'm not walking out of her life now.'

Lukas regarded her silently for a long moment. Rhiannon's heart raced and her face flamed, but she met his gaze, stony-faced and determined, her fists clenched at her sides.

'What about your own life?' he asked in a mild voice. 'Your flat, your job, your friends? If Annabel is Christos's child, her life will be in Greece. Are you prepared to move here?' He quirked one eyebrow in cynical bemusement. 'To give up everything for a child that isn't even yours…for the child of a friend you hadn't seen in ten years? A child,' he continued, his voice turning hard, unyielding, *damning,* 'that you didn't really want? A child with a family in place—a family with far more resources than you could ever possibly have?'

Rhiannon's mouth was dry, her heart like lead. When he framed it in such stark terms her situation seemed bleak indeed. 'It's not about resources,' she said stiffly. 'It's about love.'

'Can you really see yourself in Annabel's life long-term?' Lukas persisted. He kept his voice mild. 'In Greece? Are you prepared to give up your life in Wales to care for a child that is no relation to you?'

His words wound around her heart, whispered their treacherous enticements in her mind. He was trying to dissuade her from staying, she knew. From complicating his life. And yet he made sense.

If she stayed in Greece she would have a half-life at best— the life of someone who lived on the fringes of a family. Again. Yet surely it was no less of a life than she had now.

'You've done your duty,' he continued. 'You've brought her to her family. When the paternity issue is resolved, you can return to your home, your life, with a clear conscience. Isn't that what you really want? Wasn't that what you planned all along?'

His voice was so smooth, so persuasive, and it made Rhiannon realise how impossible a situation this truly was. Could she really move to Greece, ingratiate herself into the Petrakides family…if they would let her?

Yet she couldn't leave Annabel. Not like this. 'I don't…' Her mind swam, diving for words, and came up empty. 'I don't know,' she admitted. 'It's a lot to think about.'

'Indeed.' She heard the satisfaction in his voice and realised he thought he'd chipped away at her resolve. And perhaps he had. She wanted to be in Annabel's life—she wanted Annabel to be loved.

Yet how could it happen? When Lukas had all the power and she had none? When this world—his world—was so foreign to her? So *above* her?

Could she ever even remotely fit in?

Lukas kept walking, and Rhiannon followed him. The waves lapped gently at their feet.

'You said all children are inconveniences,' he remarked after a moment. 'Is that how you were viewed?'

Rhiannon's breath came in a hitched gasp. She was surprised at his perceptiveness. She stared blindly out at the ocean, dark and fathomless, a stretch of blackness, a rush of sound.

'I was adopted,' she said after a long moment. 'My parents never quite got over my arrival into their orderly lives.'

'Many adopted children have loving homes, caring parents. Was that not the case with you?'

She closed her eyes, opened them. 'My parents cared for me,' she said, choosing her words carefully. She would not tarnish their memory. 'In their own way. But I often wondered about my natural parents, and I didn't want Annabel to be the same—especially if she discovered when she was older that she could have known her father and I never gave her the chance. I wanted to spare her that pain.'

Lukas was silent for a long moment. 'I see,' he finally said.

They continued to walk, Rhiannon with sudden, quick steps as if she wanted to escape the confines of the beach, the island, the reach of this man.

He saw too much, understood too much. And yet understood nothing at all.

Lukas grabbed her arm, causing her to stumble before he steadied her, turned her to face him. 'Who are you trying to escape?' His voice was soft, almost gentle, but his hands were firm on her arms and they burned.

'I want to go back to the villa,' Rhiannon said jerkily.

'I didn't mean to upset you.' His arms moved up to her shoulders, drawing her closer. 'I was trying to understand.'

'You don't understand anything,' Rhiannon spat. 'First you judge me as a blackmailer, then as a woman who is willing to give up a child like so much rubbish.'

'I may have been mistaken in those beliefs,' Lukas said quietly. There was no apology in his voice, merely statement of fact. 'I realise now, Rhiannon, that you want what is best for Annabel. You believed that was entrusting her to her family; I think you're right.'

'I've changed my mind,' Rhiannon choked, and his hands tightened briefly on her arms.

'You must trust that I will do my duty by Annabel,' he said calmly, and Rhiannon let out a wild, contemptuous peal of laughter.

'That's the last thing I want,' she cried. 'I don't want Annabel to be bound to someone by *duty*.' It came out in a sneer, and Lukas looked at her in surprise.

'Why on earth not?'

Rhiannon drew in a shuddering breath. He was close. Far too close. So close that in the pale moonlight bathing his face she could see the gold flecks in his eyes, the stubble on his chin.

'You couldn't understand.'

'Not unless you explain,' he agreed, his voice soft yet firm in the darkness.

'I want you to let me go,' she whispered, but it didn't sound very convincing.

'I will…' Yet he was drawing her closer, and closer still, his lips a breath away from hers. Rhiannon let him hold her, let his breath fan her face, let her lips part open.

There was determination in his eyes, a fierce resolve, and Rhiannon knew that, like her, he was fighting against the tide of desire that washed over both of them, threatening to drag them under.

She knew by the light in his eyes, by the way his fingers bit into her shoulders.

And by the way he released her, suddenly, as if she'd scorched him, so she stumbled back in the sand.

'I'm sorry.' His voice was low. 'I didn't mean to start something here.'

'To kiss me?' Rhiannon challenged, irritated at how bereft she felt.

'I know nothing can happen between us,' Lukas said flatly. 'We cannot complicate matters more with a meaningless affair.'

His assessment stung. A meaningless affair? Of course he would never consider her as a worthy candidate for girlfriend, bride, wife.

She was so far below him, his world. All she was worth was an affair. Dirty, cheap. Meaningless.

'Nothing *will* happen between us,' she restated stonily. 'Because you need to do your damn duty.'

Lukas stared at her for a long moment. 'I've never had someone think so little of me for doing what is right.'

Rhiannon swallowed the guilt that rose up at his quiet words. 'I want you to *want* to do what is right,' she said. 'Not just do it out of some burdensome sense of *responsibility*.'

'You say that as if it's a dirty word.'

'It is!' Rhiannon couldn't hold back the emotion which caused her voice to tremble, her throat to ache. 'It *is*.'

They were standing only a few feet apart, tension binding them together like an invisible wire. Lukas reached out his hands, grabbed her shoulders, and pulled her towards him.

'*This* is not about duty,' he said in a savage whisper before kissing her. It was a hard, punishing kiss—a brand, a seal. When he released her they both were breathing in ragged gasps.

'But you didn't *want* that either, did you?' Rhiannon said when she finally found her voice.

'Yes,' Lukas disagreed flatly. 'The problem is, I want it too much. But I will not have it.'

He turned away, began striding down the beach. Alone in the darkness, Rhiannon had no choice but to follow him back to the distant lights of the villa.

CHAPTER FIVE

THE next morning Rhiannon avoided the dining room in exchange for some rolls, yoghurt and honey in the kitchen with Adeia.

She wanted to steer clear of Lukas after their argument last night, and so, with Annabel on her hip and a pair of towels under her arm, she headed for a secluded part of the beach. She slathered them both in suncream and then set up Annabel in a patch of sand. The baby was happy, digging busily, letting the sand trickle through her fingers, chortling with glee at the feel of it on her toes.

Rhiannon watched her, trying to ignore the ache of longing within her, the churning fear at the thought of the future. She wanted simply to enjoy the sun-kissed moment.

Lukas had been completely wrong in thinking she wanted to give Annabel away; it hurt to think he'd judged her so readily, thought so little of her.

It was the last thing she wanted. She'd fought desperately with her conscience over the matter; her heart had wanted to keep the baby, but her mind had told her the father had a right to know. A right to love.

And, her conscience had argued, wasn't it selfish for a single woman in Rhiannon's precarious financial position to keep a child she had no real right to simply because she wanted someone to love? To be loved by someone?

Wasn't it selfish and pathetic?

Yet now, she thought grimly, she might not have the opportunity. Paternity suits, custody battles...

She should have considered this sooner, she supposed. She should have thought of all the possible outcomes to confronting Lukas Petrakides. If only her heart hadn't deceived her with promises of fairy tale endings and happily-ever-afters.

She really was pathetic.

Annabel looked up, gurgled and pointed, and Rhiannon froze. She knew. She could feel him behind her, picture his easy, long-limbed stride.

'Good morning.' Lukas approached them and crouched down next to Annabel. He wore a short-sleeved white shirt and olive-green shorts. He looked clean and strong and wonderful.

Rhiannon tore her gaze away. 'Good morning.'

'Sleep well?' He gave her a questioning glance even as he held Annabel's chubby fist, poured sand into her waiting palm. She giggled in delight.

'No,' Rhiannon confessed irritably. 'Did you?'

His smile was rueful, honest. 'No.'

She was gratified by the admission, although she remained silent.

'She's a cheerful little thing, isn't she?' Lukas said after a moment, as Annabel grabbed his hands and attempted to bring one lean finger towards her open mouth. 'And teething too, I suppose?'

'Watch out—she has two front teeth, and they're sharp.'

Gently Lukas disengaged his finger from Annabel's grasp. 'Thank you.'

'If Christos *is* Annabel's father, who will look after her?' Rhiannon asked suddenly. She needed to know. An idea had begun to form in her mind—hopeless, impractical, her only chance. 'She'll need a nanny, won't she?' she continued, and Lukas regarded her shrewdly.

'Undoubtedly.'

'Better for it to be someone she knows,' Rhiannon continued, and Lukas's mouth tightened.

'Infants form attachments easily. In any case, if she is Christos's child, *I* will adopt her.'

The thought weighed as heavily as a stone on her heart. She swallowed, looked away.

Lukas laid a steadying hand on her arm. 'I realise your own adoptive parents might not have been ideal, but this will be different.'

'Oh?' Rhiannon forced herself to look at him. 'How?'

'I will care for her—' Lukas began, looking slightly, strangely discomfited.

'My parents cared for me too.' Rhiannon cut him off. 'But let me tell you, Lukas, duty is a hard parent. It doesn't kiss your scrapes better, or cuddle you at night, or check for monsters under the bed. It doesn't make you feel loved, make you believe that no matter what happens, what you do, there'll be a place to come home to, arms to put around you. Duty,' she finished flatly, 'is a cold father.' She stared blindly down at the sand, trying to rein her emotions, her memories, back under control.

Lukas's fingers grasped her chin, tilted it so she was looking at him, and she knew he could see the hurt, the pain shadowing her eyes.

'Is that how your father was?' he asked quietly. 'Your mother?'

Rhiannon shrugged. 'I don't blame them. They did the best they could.'

'But it wasn't enough, was it? And you're afraid that Annabel will suffer as you did?'

'Yes, I am,' she admitted. 'And shouldn't I be? You've already shown me what a cold, restrained person you are.'

The look he gave her was full of hidden heat. 'Have I?' he murmured, his tone so languorous that Rhiannon jerked her chin from his hand, scooted a few feet away.

'Yes. In terms of how you see your responsibility towards Annabel.'

He shrugged, spread his hands. 'I can only promise to do what is right. To give her every opportunity, every comfort.'

'That's not enough.'

'It will have to be.'

She knew it was more than most men would give—more than

she had any right to expect. But it wasn't enough. She wouldn't let it be enough.

Because she knew how duty without love became a burden, a weight. A resentment. As it had become with her. Lukas couldn't see that, couldn't understand.

A loud whirring filled the air, and Rhiannon blinked up in surprise as a helicopter came into sight.

'That's not the press, is it?' she asked, one hand shading her eyes, and Lukas shook his head.

'No, it is a Petrakides helicopter.' He pointed to the side of the craft. 'See the entwined Ps? That is our emblem.'

Rhiannon saw the entwined letters, first in the Roman alphabet, then in Greek. 'What is a Petrakides helicopter doing here?' she asked.

Lukas took her hand in his, tugged. 'Come and see.' There was a surprising smile on his face, like that of a little boy, and, scooping up Annabel, Rhiannon followed him to the landing pad.

A young Greek man emerged from the helicopter as they approached, and Lukas called a greeting. The man called back, and began unloading boxes and parcels from the body of the chopper.

Rhiannon stood back uncertainly, until Lukas beckoned her. 'Come. These things are for you.'

'For me?' she repeated blankly.

'Yes…for you and Annabel.'

He took Annabel from her, jiggling the baby on his hip, so she could inspect the parcels. Hesitantly Rhiannon opened one box to find it full of baby toys, brightly coloured, soft and enticing.

'You shouldn't have…' she began, and he shrugged her protestation aside.

'Of course I should.'

More boxes revealed clothes—play clothes for Annabel, sensible, sturdy, and well made.

'Open that one.' A faint smile curved his mouth upwards, softened his face, his eyes.

Raising her eyebrows, too curious not to obey, Rhiannon opened the box he'd indicated.

'More clothes...' Not for Annabel, though. For her. She held up a white cotton blouse—simple, flowing, with scalloped lace along its scooped neckline. She found trousers, loose and comfortable, in turquoise silk. A sundress, lemon-yellow, with skinny, flirty straps. She lowered the dress, her hands bunching in the filmy material.

'You really shouldn't have.'

'Perhaps not,' Lukas agreed quietly, his teasing little smile still flickering along her nerve endings, 'but I wanted to.'

It came out almost unwillingly, and Rhiannon found herself saying, 'You don't like to want things?'

'No, I don't,' he admitted, and there was a hardness to his tone that caused the light, happy atmosphere to evaporate. Even Annabel noticed, and squirmed in Lukas's arms.

'Why not?' Rhiannon asked, uncertainty causing her voice to waver just a little bit.

'Because wanting—giving in to your desires—causes misery and ruin. Not only for yourself, but for everyone around you.' Lukas spoke flatly. His face was hard, his eyes as flat and cold as steel. 'I've spent my life cleaning up other people's messes, paying for their mistakes. Mistakes that could have been avoided if they hadn't given in to selfish whims, desires. If they'd only done their duty—as I have done and you seem to think so lightly of.' With a curt nod, he handed Annabel back to her. 'I'll have these boxes delivered to your room. Dinner is at half past seven.'

Rhiannon pressed Annabel to her, inhaled her clean, innocent scent. She felt as if she'd just received an unexpected glimpse into Lukas's mind, perhaps even into his heart.

Who were the people he was talking about? Whose messes had he cleaned up? She could hardly ask, and she doubted Lukas would volunteer answers anyway. Yet it provided a flickering of understanding, even compassion, of why he rated responsibility so highly.

Annabel grizzled, and Rhiannon knew she needed a bottle and a nap. She headed upstairs, mind and heart still whirling.

Several hours later Annabel was fed and bathed, having spent an exhausting and enjoyable afternoon playing with her new toys.

Rhiannon gave her a bottle before settling her in the new cot—not a lightweight travel one, but a sturdy pine frame bed, with soft pink blankets.

Rhiannon knew some assistant must have picked out the clothes and toys for them. All Lukas had had to do was issue a terse order over the phone. It had been a responsibility to him, a duty fulfilled.

Yet he'd *wanted* to...

She slipped on the white blouse and turquoise trousers, admiring the silkiness of the material, the way the clothes skimmed her figure, highlighted what slight curves she had without clinging or revealing.

Her hair fell in its usual curls around her face, wild and untamed, but her eyes sparkled and her cheeks were flushed with...what? Nervousness? Expectation?

Excitement.

Lukas was waiting for her at the bottom of the stairs. He smiled when he saw how she was dressed—a smile that for one soul-splitting second lit his eyes with feral possession and made both Rhiannon's heart and her step stumble.

She grasped the wrought-iron banister, her fingers curling around it for balance.

His smile turned polite, a courtesy, and he murmured, 'I like that outfit on you.'

'Someone who works for you has good taste,' Rhiannon quipped, to give herself time to recover from that one brief, scorching look.

Lukas raised his eyebrows. 'Why do you think I hired someone to buy you clothes?'

Rhiannon checked herself. 'Didn't you?'

He shrugged. 'Maybe I chose all the things myself, on the internet, and had them flown over.'

Was he teasing? A faint blush stole across her cheeks, rendered her speechless. The idea that Lukas himself had picked out the clothes, decided what she would like, what she would look good in, *knew her size*—it was so personal, so intimate... The thought burned her as much as his touches had.

He watched her with dark, knowing eyes—eyes that knew how discomfited she was, and perhaps enjoyed it.

He said nothing, merely took her firmly by the elbow, his hand dry and warm, and led her into the dining room.

Theo stood by his chair as they entered, stiff and straight, his shoulders thrown back, a haughty look hardening his features.

Rhiannon didn't take it to heart. She knew it was not directed towards her, but was rather a defence against compassion or, worse, pity.

She smiled at the older man. He looked away.

The meal Adeia served was again delicious, and Rhiannon found she could almost relax. Theo said little, but Lukas kept up a flow of conversation about the islands, Athens, business. All fairly innocent, innocuous topics that made Rhiannon drop her guard for one treacherous moment.

Then a phone rang, trilled against Lukas's chest, and he slipped a mobile from his breast pocket. 'Excuse me… Hello?' His face darkened and he stood, turning away from Rhiannon. He spoke in rapid Greek before covering the mouthpiece of the little phone and saying, 'I need to take this privately. I beg your pardon.'

Rhiannon watched him go, her heart starting a slow, heavy thud.

Theo spoke what was already screaming through her own mind. 'That will be Christos.'

'Perhaps now,' Rhiannon said, as steadily as she could, 'we will get to the bottom of this.'

Theo's eyes glittered, and he said the one word with effort. 'Perhaps.'

The room was silent, heavy with tense expectation. Rhiannon couldn't eat, couldn't even pretend to pick at her food. Adeia cleared the plates and brought in the little cups of thick black coffee that burned down Rhiannon's throat like acid.

Still Lukas did not come.

What was going on? What was being said?

And, most importantly, what was going to happen?

Theo watched her, his eyes bright. Rhiannon tried not to let his stare unnerve her, even though her throat was dry, and she felt as if she would choke on her own words.

Finally Lukas returned, his face blank. 'Rhiannon, may I speak with you? In the study.'

'You can say it here,' Theo protested, his tone angry even though his words were halting. 'Is Christos the father?'

'I will speak to Rhiannon first. Excuse us, Papa.'

Woodenly Rhiannon followed him to a dark, wood-panelled room, with bookshelves lining all the walls except for a picture window that looked out directly onto a rocky outcropping, an unforgiving line of shore.

'That was Christos on your phone, wasn't it?' she said into the silence. 'Did he say…?'

'Yes, he did.' Lukas thrust his hands deep in his trouser pockets. 'He admitted everything. Meeting Leanne, using my name, taking her to Naxos. He repeated the story you told me almost exactly, and I hadn't even told him what you'd said.'

'It's not as if he would make it up,' Rhiannon said, her voice sounding stilted, unnatural. Why did this hurt? she wondered. It was no more than either of them had expected.

'I wouldn't put anything past Christos. He was adamant, in fact, that he had used protection, but mistakes can happen.'

'Annabel is not a mistake!' Rhiannon looked up, a fierce golden light in her eyes. She realised she was trembling.

'Not to you, perhaps,' Lukas agreed. 'But to Christos she is nothing more than that. As soon as possible I will begin adoption proceedings. Christos is delighted with the solution.' His mouth tightened briefly, and Rhiannon had a flickering of perception that Christos was not the kind of person who expressed his delight. No doubt he'd *expected* Lukas to take care of his child…his bastard. Thought it was Lukas's responsibility, as Lukas himself did.

'Obviously such action will require help on your part. As Annabel's current legal guardian, you will have to go through court to sign such rights over to me.'

Rhiannon stiffened. 'I told you, I'm staying in her life. I'm not signing anything over.'

Lukas sighed. 'Rhiannon, the last thing I want is a custody case. But Annabel is my great-niece—my blood relation.'

'Blood is so important to you?'

'Of course it is!'

Rhiannon shook her head, refusing to admit just how backed into a corner she was. 'Christos hasn't taken a paternity test yet—'

'No, but it is a mere formality now. He will take one when he returns to Athens.'

'Then we have a little time to work something out,' Rhiannon said. She drew herself up, met his gaze full-on. 'Because I don't want a court case either, Lukas, but I'm not bowing out simply because you feel you have more rights. Leanne didn't come to you when she thought you were the father. She came to me. That says something.'

'Oh?' Lukas was still—dangerously so. Rhiannon already knew what ran deep beneath those still waters. His eyes were a lethal silver, his expression like that of a predator right before it snapped open its jaws, devoured its prey. 'What does it say to you?'

'That Leanne trusted me to love Annabel.'

'Yet you were going to give her away.'

She refused to be drawn. 'I've already explained why I was prepared to do that—and, as I've said, things are different now. I'm staying.'

Lukas raised his eyebrows. 'For ever?'

Rhiannon swallowed. For ever was a long time. Yet she could hardly walk away when Annabel was older and more attached to her. She could hardly walk away at all.

'You haven't thought this through, have you, Rhiannon?' Lukas jeered softly. 'You're full of big ideas about loving Annabel, but you're not quite sure how it works out in the details. The *duties*.'

'I…'

'Because if you want to be her mother, if you want to love her, then you have to stay. You'll have to make your home in Greece. You'll have to live in the Petrakides pocket. You'll have to—' he finished with heavy emphasis '—become my responsibility…*if* I'm prepared to accept it.'

Rhiannon's mouth opened, and after a moment of silent struggling she finally choked out, 'I will never, ever, be someone's responsibility again.'

'It's not your choice.'

'It *is* my choice,' she countered fiercely. 'And just because you have an overdeveloped sense of what you're required to do in life it doesn't mean I have to fall neatly in with those plans! I'll stay in Annabel's life, but on my own terms, and not in "the Petrakides pocket", as you so snidely put it! I will provide for myself, live by myself, be completely independent...' She trailed off, running out of self-righteous steam at his look of blatant disbelief.

'That,' he said with quiet, final derision, 'is not going to happen. Do you actually think for one second that you can set up house somewhere and have me visit at weekends? My dreaded sense of duty requires a bit more action than that.'

Rhiannon pushed her hands through her hair. She wanted to slow down her whirling mind—knew she couldn't think through real solutions when her head felt as if it was spinning and her heart burned within her. 'I could be her nanny...'

'That is not your decision to make.'

'You can't cut me out of her life like this!' Rhiannon cried, her voice jagged, desperate.

'I can do whatever I want,' Lukas said bluntly. 'If you want to drag this through court, you can. But you will be bankrupted and vilified in the process. I will win any case, Rhiannon. Be assured.'

'Would you be so cruel?' she whispered, and he shrugged.

'I have Annabel's best interests at heart. I want to provide her with a secure, stable environment, and frankly I'm not sure you fit into that picture.'

Rhiannon shook her head. 'I'm not leaving until Christos takes the paternity test. We have some time to think of a plan that is beneficial to everyone.'

Lukas nodded brusquely, his face tight. 'Very well. We can speak about this later.'

Rhiannon nodded. She would have to think of a better game

plan—a clearer idea of just how she could remain in Annabel's life without being beholden to Lukas Petrakides. How he would let her.

Right now, it seemed impossible.

She opened the study door, saw Theo outside, and realised he'd probably heard every word. She couldn't summon enough emotional energy to care. Jerking her head in a nod of goodnight, she walked stiffly out of the study and up the stairs.

In her room Annabel was sleeping soundly, and Rhiannon slipped out of the silky clothes and into her old pyjamas—a tee-shirt and pair of boxer shorts. A silky nightgown, modest and yet achingly sensual, had been included in the box of clothes, but she couldn't wear something so intimate. Not if Lukas had had anything to do with the choosing.

Lukas. She couldn't escape him, couldn't run from the way he affected her. Angered her. And yet he made her ache, need. Wonder, want.

Want. Why couldn't Lukas let himself want anything? What a cold existence—to deny yourself any pleasure simply because it was pleasing to you…made you happy. Was that why he hadn't slept with a woman for two years?

There had to be a lot of sexual repression going on there. Rhiannon smothered a rueful smile. If anyone was sexually repressed, it was her. One burning look from Lukas and she was on fire. He moved towards her and she melted. She'd never reacted to any man like that. She'd never had the chance.

Like Lukas, she acknowledged, she hadn't given in to desire. Hadn't allowed herself to want. There had been no time, no opportunity. And duty to her parents had bound her with loveless cords.

Unlike Lukas, she wanted love…not duty. She wanted *more.*

Rhiannon watched the moon sift silver patterns over the floor, listened to Annabel's soft breathy sighs of sleep, and felt miles from such relaxation herself.

Her stomach growled, and she realised that she'd eaten hardly anything at dinner.

She was hungry.

She slipped out of bed, opened her door as quietly as possible.

It had to be past midnight. The house was quiet and still. Surely no one would notice—no one would mind—if she slipped down to the kitchen and grabbed a roll?

She tiptoed down the hallway, feeling strangely guilty. She stopped when she heard music.

It was coming from downstairs, floating from behind the closed door of the lounge, and it was haunting. Sad, melodious, beautiful.

Rhiannon walked downstairs, stood in front of the door, and listened. The music spoke to her soul and made her ache. Who was playing?

Stealthily, she pushed the door with the tips of her fingers and peeked in.

Lukas was at the piano, absorbed in his playing. His long, lean fingers moved gracefully over the keys, evoking that sound, that glorious emotion.

Rhiannon didn't know if she'd made a noise, or if the door had creaked, or if perhaps Lukas had just sensed her, but he looked up, his face freezing into a blank mask, his hands stilling on the keys.

'No...don't stop. It's beautiful.'

'Thank you.'

She knew that polite, impersonal tone. Knew it and hated it. She took a step into the room. 'I didn't realise you played the piano.'

'Not many people do.'

Rhiannon bit her lip. Something about that music, that soulful melody, made her want to breach his defences, to break that blank mask and find the man living, breathing, *wanting* underneath. 'Did you take lessons when you were a child?'

'No.' Lukas eased the cover over the keys. 'I taught myself.'

Rhiannon gasped in surprise; she couldn't help it. Anyone who played like that had to have natural talent, but to teach himself...? He must have been a prodigy.

'You're surprised,' Lukas remarked with a sharp little laugh. 'No doubt you think such a cold, *restrained* man shouldn't be able to play beautiful music.'

'Lukas...' Rhiannon didn't know what to say—hadn't expected him to remember her words from earlier. Hadn't thought they might hurt him. 'I always wanted to learn to play the piano,' she admitted.

'Did you have lessons?'

She shook her head, a sudden lump in her throat. She thought of the dusty piano in the front room of her parents' house, never touched, never played. It had been strictly off-limits to her.

Lukas watched her for a moment, his eyes dark, fathomless, then he slid over on the piano bench and lifted the cover up again. 'Come here.'

'Wh…what?'

He patted the seat next to him. 'Your first lesson.'

Surprised, touched, Rhiannon moved forward. She sat next to him, thigh to thigh, creating a spark of awareness deep within her.

'Here.' He placed her hands on the keys, then laid his own hands gently on top. 'This is an E.' He plucked one note, moving her own fingers. 'And this is a D.' He continued playing notes, moving her fingers, until Rhiannon recognised the tune.

'"Mary Had A Little Lamb"!'

He smiled, a flash of whiteness. 'You need to start somewhere.'

'Yes…' She was suddenly achingly conscious of his hands on hers, the closeness of their bodies, the intimacy of the moment. Her heart began to thud, desire pooled in her middle, and she could only sit there helpless. Shameless.

'Why did you come down here?' Lukas asked, breaking the moment.

'I was hungry,' Rhiannon admitted. 'I didn't eat much at dinner, and then I heard…'

'Then you should go to the kitchen.' He rose from the piano bench. 'I'll show you the way.'

She followed him into the wide, friendly room at the back of the villa, its stainless steel counter-tops and appliances softened by the colourful prints on the wall and the scrubbed pine table.

Lukas opened the refrigerator. 'What would you like?' he asked over his shoulder. 'Bread, salad, or…?' His smile glinted with sudden mischief as he brought out a plate. 'The nectar of the gods?'

He proffered a tray holding a large slice of baklava, the traditional Greek dessert, dripping with nuts and honey. Rhiannon's mouth watered.

'Definitely the nectar,' she said, and, smiling as if he had expected no less, Lukas cut her a generous slice.

She'd thought he would give it to her on a plate, with a fork. Instead he offered it to her from his own hand, lifting the filo pastry to her lips for her to take a bite.

There was a challenge in his eyes, heady, seductive, and the atmosphere changed. Just as it had before, the simple exchange turned into something potent, filled with possibilities both wonderful and terrifying.

No. This time she would not play his game. He wanted her to literally eat from his hand, and she would not do it. She knew how this ended—had experienced it before—with him thrusting her away.

She wasn't going to give herself the chance to be rejected. Again.

'Thank you.' She took the baklava from his hand and took a bite.

Lukas watched, one hip braced against the counter-top, his eyes following her movements as she self-consciously tried to eat the dessert.

Baklava was not an easy thing to eat at the best of times, and it was incredibly difficult when you had a spectator. Rhiannon was conscious of the flakes of pastry on her lips, the drip of honey on her chin.

Lukas reached out, touched the drip on her chin and licked his thumb. 'Sweet.'

'Don't.'

He raised his eyebrows, his gaze still heavy lidded, and waited.

'Don't,' she repeated, her voice a raw whisper. She set the baklava on the counter, wiped the honey from her mouth. 'You don't even *want* to. You don't even like me...'

Lukas's eyes flared with startled awareness. 'Why do you think I don't like you?' he murmured, and before Rhiannon could protest he was drawing her to him, his hands cupping her face, her head tilted back to meet his own regretful gaze. 'I fight with myself every day,' he said. 'I don't want to want you because of *me,* not because of you. Never because of you.' His lips were inches from hers. 'You drive me wild, Rhiannon. When I'm near you I can't think. I can only…' his voice came out in a jagged rasping of sound '…want.'

Rhiannon swayed towards him. She could feel the heat from his body, the desire pulsing through him, drawing her dangerously nearer.

No one had ever wanted her because of who she was, and yet here was Lukas wanting her. Wanting *her.*

Even if he didn't want to. Suddenly that didn't matter. All that she could get her head—her heart—around was that Lukas wanted her. And for that moment, with their bodies so close, yet not touching, his hands gentle on her face, it was enough.

She closed that last tempting inch, brushed her lips against his. His hands slipped up to tangle in her hair, to bring her even closer. Her arms went around him, revelling in the hardness of his chest, his shoulders, as he moulded her to him.

'Rhiannon…' he breathed against her lips. 'Rhiannon…I want you…'

She smiled against his mouth. 'You don't want anything.'

'I want *you,*' he repeated, almost savagely, and deepened the kiss. Rhiannon knew there was regret in his voice, and there was self-condemnation, but she didn't care. It was all too sweet, too wonderful, too consuming.

Her head fell back as she surrendered to the ministrations of his mouth, his tongue, his hands.

'You taste sweet,' he murmured against her skin, and she smiled.

'I was eating honey.'

'No, sweeter.' He was trailing kisses down her throat, his hands reaching under her tee-shirt to skim over her breasts, his thumbs teasing the sensitive nipples to aching peaks.

Rhiannon arched, moaned. She couldn't help it. She'd never felt so alive—every sense, every nerve ending humming, throbbing to life.

Lukas took her buttocks in his hands and hoisted her easily

onto the counter-top. Her legs wrapped around him as a matter of instinct, pulled him closer, felt his hardness at the joining of her legs, and gasped at the contact. Gasped with pleasure.

Somehow they were on top of the counter, tangled legs, bodies pressed together, his hand creeping up her thigh, nudging her old pyjama shorts aside to tease the damp curls at her femininity.

Rhiannon gasped at the intimate intrusion, the novel feeling of someone touching her where she'd never been touched before.

'All right?' Lukas murmured, looking down at her, his pupils dilated with desire, his face flushed with heat, his finger still teasing, nudging her knowingly, turning her to liquid heat.

Rhiannon opened her mouth to reply. She was about to say yes, of course she was all right. She was more than all right. Then, quite suddenly, she wasn't.

Suddenly she was aware of her rucked-up clothes, of the metal counter pressing coldly into her back, of the fact that she was lying splayed out on a chopping block like a piece of meat... And, really, wasn't she being treated like one?

Wasn't she letting herself be treated like one?

Lukas didn't love her. He didn't even *want* to be here with her. She was like a craving he had to satisfy, an itch he had to scratch, and he didn't even want to.

She closed her eyes briefly, unwilling to continue, unable to stop. She'd brought herself to this humiliating moment. She'd allowed herself to fall so far, stoop so low, simply because she wanted a little—*a little*—love.

And yet love had nothing to do with this.

Her eyes still closed, she felt Lukas pulling her shirt down. He kissed her navel, making her shiver. He tugged gently on her hand and Rhiannon slipped from the hard metal surface, her eyes open but averted.

'Look what giving in to desire does,' Lukas said, and Rhiannon heard the derision. 'Rutting like animals in the kitchen,' he continued flatly. 'No self-control at all.'

'I'll go,' Rhiannon whispered, her throat raw and tight.

Lukas had turned away from her, one hand fisted in his hair. Could he not even bear to look at her? Was he that disgusted?

'Perhaps it's best,' he said quietly, and Rhiannon fled.

Lukas waited till he'd heard Rhiannon's soft, scared footsteps on the stairs, heard the relieved click of her door. Then he swore.

He strode from the kitchen, found the lounge, and sat down at the piano—his usual source of comfort. His refuge.

Except tonight there was no escape from the torment. His body throbbed with unfulfilled desire even as his mind ached with the knowledge of what he'd stooped to…what he'd almost done.

All because of desire.

He shook his head, his fingers splaying over the piano keys without making a sound.

Desire. He'd seen it ruin lives—his mother's, his three sisters', his nephew's. All of them had given away their self-respect, their dignity, for a few moments of grasped pleasure, a mistaken belief in love.

He'd spent his life witnessing their mistakes…paying for them. He'd promised his father, and more importantly himself, that he would never give in to base cravings, no matter how strong or urgent, and watch need wreck his life.

For a brief moment he remembered his own need—a boy begging for love. Clinging, grasping, pleading…a weak, pathetic fool.

Never again.

Of course he'd had women. He was neither a monk nor a saint. But the affairs had been brief, a matter of expediency on both sides, and each time the woman he'd used—he couldn't give it a better word—had understood what she was getting.

And what she wasn't.

But Rhiannon…*Rhiannon* was off-limits. He knew that. She was innocent, vulnerable. Dangerous. An affair with her would lead to complications he didn't need, couldn't afford. He closed his eyes, imagining the tabloid headlines, the smearing of the Petrakides name.

And Rhiannon would be hurt.

He knew that—knew she was too innocent to keep herself from falling in love. Love was something he would never give. Something he would never want.

Because, as she'd reminded him, he didn't want anything. Refused to allow himself to want, to be weak.

Yet he wanted her.

Lukas swore again. Why did that slip of a woman, with too much curly hair and eyes like sunlit puddles, make him go crazy? Lose control? *Want* to lose control?

That was what chilled him the most.

Nobody made Lukas Petrakides lose control.

Nobody.

Except this one woman who had come closer than anyone else.

He stood up from the piano, strode to the window. Outside the sky was black, pricked with stars reflecting blurrily on the sea below.

He could hear the gentle lapping of the waves, the timeless sound of surf and wind, and felt soothed by the power, the effortless control of the ocean around him.

Things had to change. Rhiannon had to go. He'd wanted to give her time, to sow the seeds of doubt that would have her leaving for Wales in good conscience, thinking it was *her* idea.

Now he realised there was no time. The desire was too strong, the danger too real. Tomorrow *he* would leave...and soon so would she.

The thought of never seeing her again made Lukas's gut twist. He didn't want her to go.

The realisation shamed him. Already she was making him want, making him weak. It had to stop.

Even if it hurt. Especially if it did.

CHAPTER SIX

'YOU'RE leaving?' Rhiannon clutched the back of the chair as she watched Lukas riffle through some papers. This was the Lukas from the resort—the business Lukas, the professional man.

He wore a grey silk suit, tailored and immaculate, and he didn't even look at her as he said, 'Yes. I have business in Athens.'

'You're just going to leave me here? Like...' Her mind struggled to remember the Greek myths from his school-days. 'Like Ariadne?'

Lukas looked up, eyes glinting briefly with admiring humour. 'Ah, yes. Poor Ariadne. Theseus just left her on that island—Naxos, in fact—after she helped him slay the minotaur. A fitting comparison. Remember, though, she was rescued by Dionysus.'

'I don't want to be rescued,' Rhiannon flashed, and Lukas smiled coolly.

'No one's offering. Christos will be arriving in Athens within the week, and I need to be there.'

'I should be too...'

'No, Rhiannon,' he corrected her gently, but with ominous finality. 'That is not your place.'

'Annabel...'

'Is my responsibility.'

'Not yet!' Rhiannon retorted, eyes flashing fire, and Lukas sighed.

'Rhiannon, after all we've discussed, haven't you yet realised how impossible this situation is? I know you feel an obligation towards Annabel, an admirable desire to see her well settled, but—'

'Well *loved*,' Rhiannon corrected fiercely, and Lukas acknowledged this with a brief, brusque nod.

'You cannot possibly mean to sacrifice your career, your life, to be near her in Greece. No one requires that of you.'

No one wants that of you. That was what he was really saying. Rhiannon looked down. It had been a long, sleepless night, reliving those shaming moments in the kitchen with Lukas, her own flooding desire.

She'd also tried to think of solutions, possibilities that would keep her with Annabel.

Nothing had come to mind.

'What if I want to?' she finally whispered, and Lukas stilled.

'Don't presume,' he warned softly, 'that what happened between us last night meant...*anything.*'

'Don't flatter yourself,' Rhiannon replied, blushing painfully. 'If I choose to stay in Greece it will be because of Annabel only, not you. Last night—'

'Was a mistake.' His tone was so final, so brutal, that Rhiannon flinched.

'One you seem to keep repeating,' she finally said through numb lips.

The look he gave her from under frowning brows was dark, quelling. 'You don't need to remind me. I'm well aware of the situation—which is, in part, why I'm leaving.'

'Because of me?'

He picked up his briefcase, slid his mobile phone into his jacket pocket and stood before her, glancing down at her with something close to compassion.

'You need to let go, Rhiannon,' he said quietly, adding so she barely heard, 'And so do I.' He handed her a mobile that matched his. 'Keep this with you. I've programmed my own mobile number on speed dial. You can ring me if you run into any trouble.'

And then, with a faint whiff of his pine-scented cologne, he was gone. Rhiannon slipped the phone into her pocket, then sagged against the study chair, her hands slick on the smooth leather.

She knew she should be relieved that Lukas was gone. At least now they wouldn't be clashing. There could be no confrontations. She had a week's reprieve—a week to decide how she could stay in Annabel's life…*if* she could.

Rhiannon realised the impossibility, the sacrifice. Was it worth it? Was she willing?

She had no answers.

From upstairs Rhiannon heard Annabel's faint cries as she woke from her morning nap. She hurried up, smiled involuntarily at the sight of Annabel's dark fleecy curls and wide brown eyes peering over the edge of the cot.

'Hello, sweetheart. Shall we go to the beach this morning? Try out all your new sand toys?'

As she picked the baby up, cuddled her close, she heard the sound of a helicopter's engine throbbing to life.

Rhiannon moved to the window, Annabel on her hip, and watched the helicopter disappear into the horizon like an angry black insect.

The house suddenly seemed ridiculously silent and still.

'Come on,' Rhiannon said as cheerfully as she could, 'let's find your swimming costume.'

The morning passed pleasantly enough, and, after lunch in the kitchen with Adeia, Rhiannon put Annabel down for a nap and read one of the paperbacks Lukas had included in his box of provisions.

When Annabel woke again, she changed her and took her down to the kitchen. Adeia was busy at the stove, but had a ready smile for the baby.

'May we eat with you again?' Rhiannon asked, only to have her spirits sink when Adeia gave a vigorous shake of her head.

'Oh, no, miss,' she said in halting English. 'The master…Mr Petrakides…expects you to dine with him tonight.'

For one brief, hope-filled second Rhiannon thought the housekeeper meant Lukas. Perhaps he'd returned while she was upstairs, was waiting for her…?

The realisation of her own happiness at such a thought made her flush in shame. Of course Adeia meant Theo. And the prospect of dining alone with the sour old man made Rhiannon's spirits sink further.

She could hardly argue with the housekeeper, however, and to refuse Theo would be outright rude. With a sigh, Rhiannon set to feeding Annabel.

After giving the baby a bath and settling her for the night, she considered her own choice of clothing.

She finally settled on a pair of plain black trousers she'd brought with her, paired with the scalloped lace blouse she'd worn before.

Theo was waiting for her in the dining room. His face cracked into a rare and reluctant smile as she entered.

'I didn't think you would come.'

'That would have been rude,' Rhiannon replied with a small smile, and he acknowledged this with an inclination of his head.

'Yes…but what is a little rudeness? After all, I have been rude to you.' He spoke slowly, but there was precision to his words. Rhiannon blinked in surprise.

'I'm surprised you admit as much,' she said after a moment.

Theo shrugged, and indicated for Rhiannon to take her seat. She did so, placing the heavy linen napkin across her lap. Theo poured them both wine and sat.

'I have come to realise,' he began carefully, 'that you will be around for some time to come.'

'Oh? Has Lukas told you as much?' Rhiannon could feel her heart starting to beat faster, the adrenalin racing like molten silver through her veins. It was fuelled by hope. She forced herself to remain calm, took a sip of wine and let the velvety liquid slide down her throat.

'He has said little,' Theo admitted with a faint frown. 'But that hardly matters. I am right, am I not? You intend to stay?'

'Yes, I do.' Rhiannon met his gaze directly. Adeia entered with the first course—a traditional Greek salad of tomatoes, cucumbers, feta cheese and black olives.

'You want to be this child's mother?' Theo asked musingly, and Rhiannon felt the word reverberate through her soul. Her heart.

Mother. A real mother. Mummy.

'Legal guardian' sounded terribly cold in comparison.

'Yes,' she said, and her determination—her desire—were evident in the stridency of her tone.

Theo nodded, and Rhiannon was surprised to see a gleam of satisfaction in his eyes. What game was he playing? She'd sensed from the moment he'd rested contemptuous eyes on her that he'd wanted her gone. She was a nuisance, a nonentity.

Yet now he seemed pleased that she intended to stick around.

Why? She should be suspicious, even afraid, but the hope was too strong.

'I don't know quite how it will work out,' she began carefully, after the first course was cleared. 'Lukas doesn't seem to think there can be a place for me. But…I'm hoping to convince him when he returns from Athens.'

'He doesn't?' Theo repeated, and he almost sounded amused.

'Yes. I intend to live my own life, Mr Petrakides, as best as I can. Back in Cardiff I was a nurse, and I imagine that my credentials could in some way be transferred to Greece.' The idea had come to her that afternoon, and though she knew it was half-thought and hazy, it still gave her hope.

He raised one sceptical eyebrow. 'And the language barrier?'

'I will have to learn Greek, naturally,' Rhiannon replied with some dignity. 'I intend to anyway, for Annabel's sake. She is, after all, half-Greek.'

'Indeed.' Theo swirled the wine in his glass thoughtfully. 'And how do you suppose my son will react to such plans? You living your own life—with Annabel in your care, I presume?'

'Not necessarily,' Rhiannon said quickly. 'Annabel could remain with you—with Lukas—as long as I have visitation rights.'

It was a compromise, and one she thought Lukas might accept. She could not become someone's responsibility… Lukas's burden...even if he wanted her to. She couldn't bear to see duty turn to dread, responsibility to resentment. And she couldn't let that happen to Annabel, either.

Theo merely laughed dryly.

'We shall see what happens,' he said, his eyes glinting with humour.

Rhiannon found herself feeling both uneasy and strangely comforted by his cryptic remark.

Theo excused himself to go to bed soon after dinner.

Rhiannon noticed his pale, strained face, the way he walked slowly and stiffly out of the room. She had not broached the subject of his illness, wanting to respect his privacy, yet now it tugged at her conscience, her compassion.

With a little sigh, and realising she was lonely, she went slowly upstairs.

The mobile phone Lukas had given her was trilling insistently when she entered the room. Rhiannon hurried to it before Annabel stirred, and pushed the talk button.

'Hello?'

'I've been trying to call you for over an hour,' Lukas said, annoyance edging his voice. 'You do realise what this phone is for?'

'Yes,' Rhiannon replied. 'For me to get in contact with you. I had no idea you intended to use it the other way round.'

There was a brief pause, and then Lukas said gruffly, 'I wanted to make sure you and Annabel were all right.'

A ridiculous bubble of delight filled Rhiannon. Lukas almost sounded as if he cared. She didn't know why that should please her so much, why it made her face split into a wide smile, but it did.

Oh, it did.

'We're fine,' she said. She sat on the edge of the bed, the phone cradled to her ear. 'I had dinner with your father tonight.'

'You did?' Lukas sounded surprised. 'And you weren't on the menu?'

Rhiannon giggled; Lukas's answering chuckle made shivers of delight race along her arms, down her spine, straight to her soul. 'No, actually, I wasn't. We were both civil...more than civil.

Although…' She paused, going over the dinner conversation in her mind. 'He almost sounded like he had some kind of plan.'

'Plan?'

'For me. Us.'

'Us?' Lukas repeated thoughtfully, and Rhiannon was conscious of the intimacy, the presumption of the word. There was no 'us'.

Except right now it felt as if there was.

'I don't know. Perhaps I was reading too much into a few comments,' she said hastily.

'You don't know my father,' Lukas replied. 'He always has a plan.'

They were both silent for a moment; Rhiannon could hear Lukas breathing. There was something so intimate about a telephone conversation, she thought. A conversation just to hear voices, to connect.

A connection.

'As long as you're all right,' Lukas finally said a bit brusquely, 'I should go. It's been a long day.'

'Yes, of course.' So much for the connection. 'Goodbye,' she said awkwardly.

Lukas's voice was rough as he replied, 'Goodnight, Rhiannon.'

Rhiannon listened to the click in her ear before disconnecting herself. She laid the mobile phone on her bedside table, closed her eyes.

The maelstrom of emotions within her was confusing, potent. She shouldn't be affected by one little phone conversation—yet she was.

She was.

She wanted him. She missed him.

Rhiannon pushed herself off the bed, grabbed her pyjamas.

She would not think about Lukas. There was no point. There was no future. In a few days, weeks, everything could change. Lukas could demand she leave.

Or he could ask her to stay.

Hadn't she learned there were no fairy tale endings? Rhiannon reminded herself. Surely she wasn't dreaming…again?

* * *

She was shaken awake several hours later.

'Miss! Miss Rhiannon!' Adeia crouched next to her bed, her worn face tense and pale with anxiety. 'It's the master.'

'The master?' Rhiannon sat up, pushing her hair out of her face.

'Master Theo,' Adeia said in a high, strained voice. 'He came down to the kitchen for something to eat and he started…' She paused, baffled, searching for the word in English. 'Shaking.'

'Shaking?' Rhiannon was already slipping out of bed, throwing a dressing gown over her pyjamas. 'Where is he now? Has a doctor been called?'

'My husband Athos helped him back upstairs,' Adeia said. 'I called the doctor…he comes from the next island. He'll be here by boat as soon as he can. You said you were a nurse…?'

'Yes, I am. I'll have a look.' Rhiannon tossed a glance over her shoulder; Annabel was still asleep.

Adeia led her down the tiled hallway to Theo's bedroom, right at the end.

The room was surprisingly small and Spartan—the room of a man who had never grown accustomed to luxury. Theo lay in bed, still and silent.

Rhiannon approached the bed. He looked even more care-worn than he had this evening—smaller, somehow, more fragile. Rhiannon's heart gave a strange little twist and she laid her hand on the old man's brow.

His eyes flickered, then opened. 'What…what are you…?' he said in a weak, halting voice.

'You had a seizure,' Rhiannon informed him quietly. 'Adeia called me. I'm a nurse.'

'I want…' He swallowed, started again. 'I want a doctor.'

'The doctor's been called. He'll be here shortly. In the meantime, I'm just going to check your vitals.'

Theo glared at her, too weak to resist, and Rhiannon gave him a small encouraging smile as she quickly checked him over. He seemed all right, she decided, while at the same time acknowledging to herself the seriousness of a man Theo's age having a seizure.

* * *

Dawn was edging the sky when the doctor's boat scraped against the island's dock, and Rhiannon's eyes were gritty with fatigue.

She'd kept watch by Theo's bed, in case there was anything to report to the doctor. She'd watched him drift in and out of sleep, his eyes glazed, and knew she would have to ring Lukas.

'He's stable for now,' the doctor told her in a low voice after he'd seen Theo. 'As the tumour affects more parts of his brain, more aspects of his life will be affected.' He paused, his expression sober. 'He knows this...knows it will continue to get more difficult.'

Rhiannon nodded. It was no more than she'd expected, and yet it still hurt. It always hurt to hear of someone's pain, the suffering of watching a life slip slowly—or not so slowly—away.

'What should we expect now?' she asked.

The doctor shrugged. 'More seizures, some lessened mobility, increased difficulty in talking. You are his nurse?'

'Not...not exactly,' Rhiannon replied, surprised. 'I mean, I am a nurse, but not...'

The doctor looked nonplussed. 'You're here; you're a nurse. I don't see many others around. If you have questions, you may ring me. All you can really do is make him comfortable. We are managing his decline.'

Rhiannon nodded and thanked him, before heading upstairs with a heavy heart. She waited until Annabel was fed and dressed and busy with Adeia before ringing Lukas.

He answered on the first ring. 'Rhiannon? Is something wrong?'

'Lukas...' Her voice came out thready. She stopped, started again. 'Lukas, your father had a seizure last night.'

There was a moment of silence, frozen, tense, and then Lukas repeated blankly, 'A seizure?'

'The doctor came. He said your father's stable for now, but...'

'But?' Lukas repeated softly.

'But,' Rhiannon admitted, 'his condition is likely to deteriorate more rapidly from now on.'

There was another silence; Rhiannon's heart ached. She

longed to comfort him, to put her arms around him. The realisation surprised her with its sorrowful power.

'I'll come back,' Lukas said finally. 'I should have been there.'

'There was nothing—'

'I should have been there.' His voice was flat, dead. 'Goodbye, Rhiannon. Thank you for telling me.'

Yet another responsibility Lukas had put on himself, she thought as she put down the mobile. Another burden weighing him down.

No man deserved so much heaped on his shoulders.

Lukas arrived by helicopter just a few hours later. Rhiannon watched from her window, Annabel playing at her feet. He went straight to his father; she heard his quick footsteps on the stairs. She wondered when—if—he would come to see her.

He'd left the island to escape her. She doubted he was in any hurry to see her again now.

'You shouldn't have come back.'

Theo's voice was thready, weak, and Lukas tried not to let his shock show on his face. His father looked half the man he had been only a day ago as he lay in bed, his usually thick shock of white hair thin and flat against his head.

'Of course I should have,' he replied evenly. 'You're my father.'

'I'm fine.' Theo spoke in fits and starts, his voice slightly wheezy. At times he struggled for over a minute for a certain word or phrase.

It made Lukas ache to hear his father like this—to see a man who held the deeds to the most desirable real estate in all of Greece in one triumphant fist reduced to such weakness and misery.

'There was business to attend to,' Theo continued with effort.

'I've seen to it.' Lukas stared blindly out of the window. 'Is the doctor acceptable? We can hire a nurse, of course. One of the best from Athens.'

Theo shook his head.

Lukas heard the movement, the rustling of covers, and turned. 'What?'

'I have a nurse.'

It took a moment for him to realise, and then he stared at his father in surprise. 'You mean Rhiannon?'

Theo nodded. 'She suits me.'

It was the last thing he'd expected his father to say. To admit.

'And,' Theo continued in a stronger voice, 'she suits you too.'

This shocked Lukas all the more. His face went blank and he turned back to the window. 'I don't know what you mean.'

'You do.' It was all Theo could afford to say, yet somehow it was enough.

Lukas was silent, but a familiar restless energy was now pulsing through him. *She suits me.* Yes, she did. All too well. Yet he could not give in to the desire, the need. He knew where that led, had seen the destruction.

The weakness.

'Marry her, Lukas.'

He swivelled, stared in shock. 'What? You are joking.'

Theo shook his head. 'No.'

'You know I've said I'll never marry.'

'I know. But now…Annabel…she needs a family.'

'She'll have one—'

'Not some patched affair!' Colour rose in Theo's gaunt face. 'A real family. I'd rather pass this company on to a girl who grew up in a loving home than to a drunken lout like Christos. Marry her, Lukas.'

Lukas shook his head. 'But it would not be a *loving* home.'

Theo's eyes brightened shrewdly. 'Wouldn't it?'

He stiffened, turned back to the window. 'I can't.'

'Why not?'

The room was silent save for Theo's laboured breathing. 'I can't allow…' Lukas stopped, shook his head. He wouldn't go there. Wouldn't admit the truth. 'Because she wouldn't have me,' he finally said, shrugging carelessly.

'What?' Theo was so surprised he laughed. 'What—what woman wouldn't have you? You, the most desirable bachelor in all of Greece? Pah. Of course she'll have you.'

'You don't know her.'

'I don't need to. If not for you, then for Annabel. She'll do it for the child.'

The child. Would she? Instinctively Lukas knew she would…if she were given the right incentives, the right words.

He could have her.

It was too tempting, too dangerous. Too possible.

And yet…he wouldn't love her. Wouldn't allow himself that luxury, that weakness. But he could have her, enjoy her, and make her life better than whatever pathetic existence she'd had in Wales.

It could happen. He could make it happen. He saw his father watching him with bright, shrewd eyes and he jerked his head in the semblance of a nod.

'We won't talk about this again.'

'As you wish.'

Rhiannon scrambled up from the sand as Lukas approached. Annabel was playing happily next to her with some new toys, but she clapped her hands in delight when she saw Lukas's long-legged stride down the beach.

'You saw Theo?' Rhiannon asked, and Lukas nodded.

'Yes.' He paused, his mouth a hard, unwilling line. 'He's not well.'

'No, he isn't.'

'I didn't expect…' He shrugged. 'Thank you for your care of him.'

'I was glad to do it.'

'My father has taken a liking to you,' Lukas said. 'He would like you to continue as his nurse, as time allows.'

'I would be happy to,' Rhiannon replied, and realised she spoke the truth. Caring for Theo would give her a purpose on this island besides waiting for results. Answers. Perhaps it would extend her stay?

'This…changes things,' Lukas said slowly. 'As long as my father has need of you I would like you to stay.'

'Of course.'

'Perhaps…' He spoke carefully, choosing his words. 'Perhaps it will give us time to think of alternative solutions.'

'I have thought of something—'

Lukas held up one hand. 'We will discuss this later. The doctor is coming back tomorrow. I've arranged for him to take a sample of Annabel's blood for the paternity test. I know it's only a matter of form now, but it's still necessary.'

Rhiannon nodded. 'Fine.'

Lukas dug his hands in his pockets. 'When does Annabel nap?'

'After lunch. Why…?'

'We'll talk then.'

After Annabel had been settled in, Rhiannon found Lukas in his study, half buried in papers. He looked up as she peeked cautiously around the door.

'Rhiannon!' His smile was, quite simply, devastating. Rhiannon wasn't used to such a fully-fledged grin, showing his strong white teeth and the dimple in his cheek. For a moment he looked happy, light, without care.

Then the frown settled back on his mouth, his brows, and on every stern line of his face. It was the look she was used to—the look she expected. Yet for one moment she hadn't seen it, and now she wanted it banished for ever.

The thought—the *longing*—scared her with its force.

'I have asked Adeia to watch Annabel,' he said, and Rhiannon blinked in surprise.

'Are we going somewhere?'

'Yes. You'll need a hat…and a swimming costume.'

Rhiannon's brows rose. 'I thought we were going to talk!'

'We are, but I'd much prefer to do it in pleasant surroundings, enjoying ourselves,' Lukas said. 'Wouldn't you?'

Yes, she would. Even if it was a mistake. A temptation. 'All right. I'll get my things.'

Her heart was fluttering with a whole new kind of fizzy anticipation as she slipped on a bikini and topped it with the yellow sundress Lukas had bought her. There was a wide straw hat to match the dress, with a yellow ribbon around its crown, and strappy sandals that were practical enough to manage the beach.

Rhiannon didn't know where they were going, what they would do—what would happen—but she liked feeling excited. The prospect of an afternoon with Lukas seemed thrilling, even if they were going to have that dreaded 'talk'.

'You look lovely,' Lukas said when Rhiannon returned downstairs. He gestured to the picnic basket on one arm. 'I had Adeia pack us a hamper.'

'All…all right,' Rhiannon stammered, suddenly unnerved by what looked like all the trappings of a romantic date.

He led her not to the beach, as she'd anticipated, but to the dock.

Along with a speedboat for travelling to the nearest island, an elegant sailboat rested there. It was this craft that Lukas indicated they should board.

'We're going to sail?' Rhiannon said dubiously. 'I've never…'

'Don't worry.' Lukas's smile gleamed as he stretched out one hand to help her on deck. 'I have. And we'll stay away from the press.'

He certainly had sailed before, Rhiannon thought, when she was perched on a seat in the stern of the boat, watching with blatant admiration as Lukas prepared the sails and hoisted the jib. Every time he raised his arms she saw a long, lean line of rippling muscle that took her breath away.

This felt like a date, she thought, as Lukas smiled at her over his shoulder. Lukas was relaxed, carefree, a different man.

Why? Was she paranoid to be suspicious? To doubt this change in events, in mood?

She didn't want to doubt. She wanted to enjoy the sun, the afternoon. Lukas.

'What are you thinking?' Lukas asked as he came to sit next to her once the boat was cutting a clear path across the blue-green sea.

'How we both need this,' Rhiannon admitted. 'A day away from the stresses and troubles back home.'

'Home, is it?' he murmured, without spite, and she flushed.

'For now, I suppose.'

'What was your home like growing up?' As always he'd switched topics—and tactics—so quickly Rhiannon could only blink in surprise. 'I know you were adopted, and it wasn't very happy, but...' He trailed off, spreading his hand, one eyebrow raised. 'Tell me about it.'

'There isn't much to tell,' Rhiannon replied, careful to keep any bitterness from her voice. 'I was abandoned when I was three weeks old. Left on a church doorstep, actually. My mother—my adoptive mother, I mean—arranged flowers for the church and she found me. I'd only been left a little while, she said, or she would have been afraid of what the squirrels might've done to me.'

Lukas's lips pursed briefly in distaste before he continued, 'Did she make any effort to find your mother or father?'

'No. Mum always said anyone who would leave a baby like that didn't deserve to have one. I used to dream...' She hesitated. 'I used to imagine them coming to look for me. I had all sorts of reasons why they might have abandoned me.' She smiled ruefully; it hurt, so she shrugged. 'Anyway, she and Dad adopted me— Social Services were happy to comply. Mum and Dad were upstanding members of the community, so everything was in order.'

'But you never really felt they wanted you?' Lukas finished, and Rhiannon flinched.

'I've never said that!'

His tone was gentle, his eyes soft and silver with compassion. 'You've never needed to.'

Rhiannon looked away, across the flat surface of the sea, glittering as if a thousand diamonds had been cast upon its waters. She hunched one shoulder. 'They were older when they adopted me. Late forties. They'd never expected to have children. Mum couldn't.'

'All the more reason to be overjoyed when they were given a chance with you, I would have thought.'

She shrugged. 'I suppose by the time I came along they were well set in their ways. A little toddler can be a burden, I know.'

'And you felt like one?'

'They never said it,' Rhiannon protested, almost desperate to exonerate their memory. 'It was just…there.' She paused, remembering all the moments, the pursed lips, the disapproving looks. The feeling that if she could just act as if she wasn't there, perhaps they'd love her.

Silly to think that way now, she knew. Yet that was how she'd thought when she was six, twelve, twenty-two.

'I remember one time,' she began, the memory rushing back with aching sorrow, 'I was hungry. Mum strictly forbade snacking between meals, but I'd missed lunch at school for some reason—I can't remember now. She was out at a flower guild meeting, and I made myself a sandwich. I cleaned up afterwards, so she wouldn't even know, but there was a drip of brown sauce on the worktop, and she was…furious.' Rhiannon managed a rueful smile. 'No dinner for me that night.'

She was surprised to feel Lukas's hand on her shoulder, slipping up to cup her cheek. 'I'm sorry.'

'Don't be.' She leaned against his hand; she couldn't help it. The strength, the security radiating from him, from that simple gesture, were overwhelming. 'It was a long time ago.'

'But the scars are still there?'

'Yes, I suppose they are.' She thought of her mother's pain-worn face on her sickbed, of how she'd cared for her endless day after endless day. Her mother had accepted those ministrations with pursed lips and hard eyes, glaring resentfully at the daughter whom she somehow blamed for her reduced circumstances.

She'd asked her mother once, right before she had died, if she'd loved her.

Her mother's mouth had tightened as she'd admitted unwillingly, 'I tried.'

Tears stung Rhiannon's eyes, surprising her. She was past tears. These were old memories, and she didn't like Lukas bringing them up.

She moved away; Lukas dropped his hand. 'Tell me about yourself, Lukas. You mentioned that you clean up after other people's messes. What's that about?'

His face blanked for a second, and she was afraid he wasn't

going to tell her, that this wonderful moment of intimacy—an intimacy she'd never expected to share with him—was over. Then he shrugged.

'My mother left my father when I was five. She fell in love with another man—someone totally unsuitable. A racing car driver. And he lived life like he raced cars. Fast.'

'And?' Rhiannon prompted softly.

'They were killed in a car crash when I was nine. It taught me a lesson.' He could still hear his father's hard voice. *See where giving in to desire leads you. See what happens when you believe in love rather than duty.*

And he could hear his mother—her careless, mocking voice. He could hear his own pleas and they shamed him.

'What lesson was that?'

'She followed her own selfish desires—didn't think about what her responsibilities were to her husband, her children. Look where it led her.' He held up a hand to stop Rhiannon's comment. 'And my three older sisters have followed her path. Antonia, Christos's mother, is divorced, she's been in rehab half a dozen times, and is a wreck. Daphne is single, miserable, parties too much and is constantly getting in trouble with the press. And Evanthe, the youngest, is anorexic and has been suicidal in the past. All because of giving in to desire. Lust. What they call love. It made them weak, pathetic.' As he had once been, and would never be again. He shook his head in disgust before glancing at Rhiannon. 'Now do you see?'

'I see,' Rhiannon answered quietly. What she saw was three women desperate for love, who'd looked for it in all the wrong places. If she'd been given the chance, if her life had gone differently, perhaps she would have been the same.

Was that what she was doing here?

The question came so suddenly that Rhiannon jerked back in surprise.

No, surely not? Surely she wasn't falling in love with Lukas? Surely she wasn't so pathetic, so foolish, so naïve?

So desperate.

Yet she realised she *was* desperate. Desperate for love, for affection, for touch. All the things she'd never had from her parents. All the things she'd known she wanted somehow, some way. With someone.

Just not Lukas. Not from a man who prided himself on being emotionally unavailable, who saw love as a needless, harmful emotion—a selfish whim! Lukas only saw in terms of black or white, duty or desire.

There was no in-between, no room to negotiate, and certainly no room to fall in love.

'What?' Lukas raised one eyebrow, and Rhiannon realised that she had an appalled look on her face. 'What is it?'

She tried to relax her face into a smile. 'I'm sorry for your family,' she said after a moment. 'There has been a great deal of sorrow.'

'Needless sorrow,' he said, his tone hardening, and Rhiannon was reminded of the untold part of Lukas's story. His sisters might be desperate for love, but then, as a boy, surely Lukas had been too?

He'd learned to ignore it, to disregard it. No doubt his father had drilled into him the wastefulness of his mother's and sisters' lives, the importance of duty.

As he'd already said, he was still cleaning up their messes. No doubt running interference with the press, paying debts, trying to keep the Petrakides name untarnished.

All by himself.

Her heart ached—ached for the boy he had been, watching his mother leave him at only five years old, and for the man he'd become. A man who couldn't love, couldn't trust, because he was afraid.

The idea of Lukas being afraid of anything seemed ridiculous, laughable, and yet in her heart Rhiannon knew it was true. He was afraid to love, afraid to be vulnerable, afraid it would lead to ruin.

'Enough of this sad talk,' Lukas said. He reached for the hamper Adeia had packed. 'I didn't come here to talk about the past, but the future. First we eat.'

Rhiannon was glad for the reprieve. The sea air had whetted

her appetite, and she wasn't quite ready to jump into a talk about the future—especially when their discussion of the past had brought so many uncomfortable memories churning to the fore.

Lukas brought out a dish of black olives, a tomato and feta salad, and some crusty bread. They both dug in with gusto.

'There isn't anything nicer than this,' Rhiannon said after a moment. 'Sitting in the sun, in the middle of the sea, eating delicious food.' With a delicious man. She kept that last thought to herself, although she felt her cheeks warming.

'Paradise,' Lukas agreed.

They finished their bread and salad in silence, and then Lukas brought out another covered dish.

'I saved the best for last.' He opened it, revealing a heavenly slice of baklava.

Rhiannon stared at the sticky sweet, her cheeks flaming. She couldn't quite meet Lukas's eyes.

'Adeia packed forks,' he said with wry humour, and an unwilling laugh escaped her.

'Good. Much easier that way.'

Lukas's gaze was thoughtful as he handed her a plate. 'It certainly is…although less enjoyable, perhaps.' And she knew they were not just talking about eating dessert. The memory of that intimacy was heavy and expectant between them.

They finished their baklava in silence. Afterwards Lukas put away the dishes and turned the sail for home.

The wind had quietened down, and the boat drifted slowly, lazily, along the water. Rhiannon trailed a hand through the foamy wake.

'Now,' Lukas said gently, settling himself beside her once more, 'we talk.'

She looked up through her lashes, took a breath. 'You sound like you have plan.'

'I do.'

Her heart began a heavy bumping against her ribs. 'I have a plan too,' she said. 'I've been thinking…' She hesitated at Lukas's carefully blank look.

'Tell me about it,' he said, after a long moment.

Rhiannon took a breath. 'I realise Annabel needs to grow up as a Petrakides. If I can be in her life, I'm willing to take a smaller role.'

'Are you?' Lukas asked, and she didn't like the dangerous neutrality of his tone.

'Yes. I could live in Athens—transfer my qualifications, learn Greek. If I could visit Annabel a few times a week…'

'You'd be willing to completely rearrange your life for a few hours a week?' Lukas asked, and there was both disbelief and condemnation in his tone.

'Why not? You're not willing to have me be *more* involved, are you?' Rhiannon lifted her chin. 'Over and over you've made it clear *you* will decide Annabel's future, and there's been more than a suggestion that I'm not involved! But you can't stop me from moving to Athens, Lukas.'

Lukas shook his head. 'This is not how I wanted to talk. Rhiannon, there need not be enmity between us. I've come to realise you care for Annabel. I do not doubt your sincerity…'

'But…?' Rhiannon prompted, a bitter edge to her voice. Lukas was silent. When she looked at him, his gaze was grey and steady, his face calm and yet filled with determination.

'There is another solution—one that I believe will be amenable to both of us.'

'What is that?'

'Marry me.'

CHAPTER SEVEN

RHIANNON could only stare, those two tempting, unbelievable words echoing in her mind.

'Marry you?' she finally choked out.

Lukas replied, steady as ever, 'It would be good between us.'

She shook her head, and spoke the only word, the only question, clamouring in her mind. Her heart. 'Why?'

'Because it makes sense. Because it's the right thing to do.' He spoke so calmly, so sensibly—and every instinct in her rebelled. If she'd had a moment's heady temptation—a moment's weakness—it was gone.

'Those are not good reasons to marry you, Lukas.' She drew her knees up to her chest, hugged them.

'They're very good reasons,' he replied evenly. 'Although perhaps not the ones you want.'

'You know what I want?'

He shrugged. 'No doubt you want some fairy tale fantasy. You want me to admit that I've fallen in love with you, that I can't live without you, that I must have you as my bride.' Each declaration was a sneer. A wound.

His smile was twisted, tinged with bitterness. 'You want me to act as a lovesick swain, a foolish, foppish boy, and that is not who I am.'

'There is a difference between being in love and being lovesick,' Rhiannon said. 'But this isn't about what you want or what I want, is it? It's about your wretched duty.'

'And yours,' Lukas countered. 'Something I've noticed about you, Rhiannon—you don't want to be anyone else's responsibility, but you're quick to assume your own. I thought at first you were trying to palm Annabel off—' he held up both hands to ward off her furious denial— 'but now I know you weren't. You were trying to do your duty, just like you did with your parents. I can't imagine it was pleasant, nursing people who'd never loved you. I doubt they even gave you a thank-you.'

Rhiannon stiffened. She hated his perceptiveness, hated the way he gazed at her so calmly, as if he had not peeled away her secrets mercilessly, one by one. As if he hadn't just asked her to spend the rest of her life with him! He wasn't the least bit unnerved, and yet she felt positively unhinged.

'I did what I needed to do,' she agreed after a moment, 'because it was my responsibility. I was their daughter.' She drew in a breath, met the force of his magnetic penetrating gaze. 'But it is not my responsibility to marry you, Lukas. We don't even know if Christos is Annabel's father—'

Lukas waved her protestation aside. 'He admitted it, and Leanne named him as the father, even if she thought he was me. A paternity test will only confirm what everyone already knows—what we can see with our own eyes.'

Rhiannon shook her head. 'We can provide for Annabel another way. A better way. A loveless marriage can hardly benefit her.'

'Would it be so loveless?' Lukas's eyes glinted, and the breath was momentarily robbed from Rhiannon's lungs.

'What are you saying?' she demanded, and he shrugged, unapologetic.

'I'm not saying I love you, or you love me. But there is a passion between us, Rhiannon. You cannot deny that.' To prove his point he leaned forward, ran his fingers along her bare shoulder.

Rhiannon shivered. She wished she could control it, wished he didn't affect her so damn much. But she couldn't, and he did.

'Agreed,' she said, her voice shaking only a little bit. 'But that's not enough. For me.'

Lukas was silent for a moment. 'Sometimes you need to

accept what's given and realise it's the most you can have. Rhiannon, there is desire between us. In time affection, friendship. It is more than most people have. It is a strong basis for marriage. Can't it be enough for you?'

She shook her head, unable to deny, to confess. She wanted more. She wanted to be Annabel's mother, or as good as, and she wanted to be loved.

By Lukas.

The realisation hurt. It made her weak, vulnerable, needy. All the things Lukas believed love did to you.

And it did.

'I won't.' It came out in a wretched whisper. 'I won't *settle*. I've settled my whole life, accepted what little I was given, and I admit it now—I want more. More.' She lifted her head, met his cool gaze with blazing eyes. 'I want to be loved, Lukas. For who I am. I want to be with someone who can't imagine life without me, who needs me, who *knows* he needs me. Someone who accepts me and cherishes me.' She saw something flicker in his eyes—disgust? Pity?—and lifted her chin. 'I suppose that seems pathetic to someone like you, who gets by with cold duty as your companion.'

Lukas didn't reply for a moment, his expression shuttered and distant. 'No,' he finally said, and she was surprised at the regret and sorrow lacing his words. 'It's not pathetic. Just unrealistic.' He shook his head and shrugged, forcing a smile to his lips. 'There is time. We do not need to decide anything now.'

Alarm fluttered in her middle, and Rhiannon realised it was mixed with anticipation. It would be all too easy for Lukas to chip away at her resolve. She might say she wanted more, but she knew she was already falling for him, for the careless and calculated crumbs of affection he tossed her way. She wanted more, but she might accept little. For Annabel's sake. For her own.

'Enough talk for now,' Lukas said. 'Let's swim.'

Lukas directed the boat to a secluded cove on the island, out of view of the main house. He dropped anchor, took off his shirt, and dived into the water.

As he surfaced Rhiannon found her heart thumping far too loudly at the sight of his chest, bare and brown, with sparkling rivulets of water streaming down that lean, tanned flesh.

He slicked his hair back with his hands and raised one arrogant eyebrow. 'Coming in?'

It was a challenge, and one Rhiannon wouldn't refuse. 'All right.' She slipped off her sundress, conscious of how her bikini emphasised the slightness of her curves. There was only admiration in Lukas's gaze as he watched from the water and, emboldened, Rhiannon stepped onto the side of the ship and neatly dived in.

When she surfaced, Lukas was smiling. 'I didn't even ask if you could swim.'

She laughed, treading water. 'I wouldn't have dived in if I couldn't! That was one happy aspect of my childhood...living near the sea.'

'Your parents took you?'

'School trips mostly,' Rhiannon admitted. 'Sometimes they took me, though.'

He nodded in understanding, and then began to swim with long, even strokes to the shore. 'Let me show you the beach,' he called over his shoulder.

Rhiannon followed him, swimming to the shore. Lukas helped her out of the shallows, kept hold of her hand as he led her onto the beach.

'There's a legend,' he said, his fingers twined with hers, 'that pirates took a mother from this island about a thousand years ago. She was forced to leave her child, but as they passed the church where she used to light a candle, she prayed for salvation.'

'What happened?'

'The ship stopped. The pirates were amazed—and, naturally, frightened. When they realised why the vessel had stopped moving—because of a mother's prayer—they brought her back to the shore, back to her baby. It's considered a miracle.'

Rhiannon wondered why he'd told her that particular legend. Did he see parallels between that mother and her own desperate situation?

Would she be forced to leave the island? Leave Annabel?

But Lukas had given her an option to stay. Marry him.

Why? she wondered. Why did he want to marry her? Was it simply for desire's sake? Or was there another reason? One she couldn't begin to guess?

They'd walked the length of the beach, and now stopped before a rocky outcropping. 'The house is just over these rocks,' Lukas said. 'When I was a boy we spent our summers here. I used to clamber over those rocks and come here.' His smile was rueful, but Rhiannon thought she saw a hidden sadness in his eyes. 'No one could find me here.'

'You didn't want to be found?'

'Sometimes, no.'

Rhiannon could just imagine it. A boy without the love of his mother, saddled with more weight and responsibility than any grown man should have, already learning the futility and weakness of love, hardening his heart and his soul.

No wonder he'd occasionally wanted to escape it all.

For a moment her heart ached for that boy, the boy underneath the tough exterior now, and she wondered if Lukas could learn to love again. Learn to trust.

If he could...if that boy truly did still exist under the man...could he love? Could he love *her?*

Rhiannon swallowed. Already she was wondering, weakening. Wanting.

'We should go back,' she said after a moment, when the only sound was the whisper of the waves on the sand and their own soft breathing. 'It's getting dark.' And her thoughts were twisting away from her, turning into impossible hopes, ridiculous dreams.

She couldn't afford to let that happen.

The sun was starting to sink in the horizon, turning the surface of the sea to shimmering gold, and, still holding her hand, Lukas tugged her back towards the sailboat.

'Are you up for another swim?' he asked, indicating the distance to the boat.

Rhiannon shrugged. 'Why not?'

She plunged into the sea after Lukas, watched as he cut through the water ahead of her and lifted himself easily onto the boat.

He'd let a rope ladder down the side, but trying to get her balance in the water, with the ladder jerking under her hands, was more difficult than she'd anticipated, and she began to fall helplessly back.

'Here...let me.' Lukas reached down, put his hands under her arms and hauled her up.

Tumbling forward, Rhiannon found herself pressed against the wet length of him—with very little material between them.

'I'm...I'm sorry,' she stammered, and his eyes glinted with humour as he held her to him.

'I'm not.'

Rhiannon's breath leaked from her lungs as that knowing glint turned from humour to desire. Lukas smoothed a damp tendril of hair from her forehead, caressed her cheek.

'Rhiannon...'

She knew what was going to happen—knew it in her bones, in the melting liquid core of her, in her heart.

The moment's silence was a question, and Rhiannon answered it by reaching up, letting her hands curl around his bare slick shoulders.

Lukas bent his head, kissed the salt from the hollow of her throat. Rhiannon moaned her acceptance, her need.

Her desire.

He kissed her lips softly. A tender promise. Rhiannon let her hands slide through his hair, damp and curling, let herself be laid down on the padded bench, with Lukas sliding his hands down her sleek, wet body.

'You are so beautiful.' His voice was ragged, uneven. 'I want you so much.'

She knew what a confession it was—for him to admit it, and to do so without shame. Without regret. Right now she felt only desire, want, need. It felt good. It felt right.

Smiling, she brought his face to hers, let their tongues tangle as he explored every soft hollow, every slender curve.

His hand cupped her breast, his thumb stroking her nipple

through the fabric of her bikini to an aching peak. She slid her own hands down his chest, loving the hard, lean feel of him, yet not quite daring to let her hands slide further down to the pulsing heat at her middle. She was too naive, too nervous.

He smiled against her mouth. 'Touch me.'

Emboldened, she did, her hand skimming across the top of his swimming trunks before darting back at the feel of his hardness.

She felt every inch the shy virgin, but wished she didn't. Wished she was confident in her desire of him, his desire of her. Yet she wasn't, she knew. She was caught up in the moment, afraid to think. Almost afraid to feel.

Yet wanting it so much.

He chuckled. 'Let me show you.'

She didn't know quite what he meant until she felt the scrap of her bikini bottom being nudged away, his fingers brushing between her legs. She gasped as he stroked her knowingly, tenderly, and then gasped again—louder—as his finger slid inside her warm heat.

She'd never felt so consumed, so known, so much a part of something bigger and more wonderful than herself.

So loved.

His fingers moved with deft assurance, knowing her secret spot, the sensitive nub, and stroking it with tender purpose.

Lukas's lips curved in a knowing smile as Rhiannon arched helplessly against him, craving his touch, craving more.

His finger began to slide and stroke in rhythm, and, still in thrall, Rhiannon moved against him, gasping out loud.

'Lukas…'

'Let yourself feel, Rhiannon. Let yourself go.'

She shook her head, as if to deny the feelings—deep, wonderful, molten—spiralling within her to a crescendo she could not even name.

'Lukas…'

'Let yourself,' he commanded gently, brushing her lips in a kiss.

And she did. She cried out loud, a choking sob of pleasure as he brought her to that glorious crescendo, more heartbreaking and real and vibrant than anything she'd ever experienced before.

Her muscles convulsed around his finger and her head fell back against the arm that cradled her head.

'I never...'

'I know.'

She laughed shakily. 'I suppose you do.'

She should have felt vulnerable, exposed. Shamed. She'd expected to—because she knew he didn't love her. She knew this was just sex.

Yet she wouldn't let herself think that way. Wouldn't allow her mind to wander down that treacherous path to its shameful destination.

She just wanted to feel...wanted. She wanted to enjoy it.

Still, she was conscious of the chill in the air, of the water cooling on her skin, her swimming costume still in disarray.

Lukas was staring at her with a teasing smile, a smile that reached deep inside her and grabbed hold of her soul. Her heart.

She *wanted* this man. She thought of his offer of marriage and realised she was tempted...far too tempted.

Lukas replaced her bikini bottoms, his smile turning knowing. 'You'll marry me now,' he said with smug satisfaction, and Rhiannon stiffened.

The feelings she'd denied rushed over her in an icy wave...vulnerable, exposed, ashamed.

She struggled to a sitting position, tugged hopelessly at her swimming costume.

'Are you telling me you planned that little scene to convince me to marry you?' Her voice came out on a shaky waver.

Lukas shrugged, his expression hooded. 'You can't deny what's between us.'

Rhiannon shook her head. 'Don't manipulate me, Lukas.'

'Is that what I was doing?' His eyebrows rose; his expression was cool. 'You seemed to enjoy it.'

'That's not fair.' She struggled to keep her tone calm, reasonable. 'Don't use sex as a way of getting what you want.'

'Don't call something you agreed to with every fibre of your being manipulation!' Lukas replied, with a dangerous chill in his tone. 'You want me, Rhiannon, and I want you. It's that simple. Want.'

'You don't want anything,' Rhiannon flashed, and his smile was bitter.

'No, I don't. And, damn it, I didn't want to want you. But I do, and I admit it. I want you,' he continued with cold precision, 'and I will have you.'

'Don't order me around!'

'You want me too,' Lukas said flatly. 'Even if you think you're holding out for some absurd notion of what love is.'

'You don't know what love is!' Rhiannon cried, and Lukas's smile was bitter.

'Oh, yes, I do. And that's why I'll never love you, or anyone, again. We can have something much better than love, Rhiannon. We can have trust, affection, desire. Something real. Something to build on. We don't need love. Love makes a fool of you, a weakling, a slave.'

She shook her head wearily, then laid it on her knees. She couldn't continue this conversation. Couldn't explain to Lukas how it might make sense now, this marriage, but what about in a year? Five years? Ten?

How long would it take for resentment to lodge in his soul, in his heart? For any affection and desire they might have shared to turn into anger and bitterness because they'd really only married for the sake of a child, and not even one they could call their own?

She wanted more for Annabel. More for herself.

'Who made a fool of you?' she asked quietly, when the silence had gone on too long.

Lukas's face closed in on itself like a fan. He shook his head. 'Let's go home.'

Silently, every movement terse and controlled, he set sail for home. Rhiannon watched the first stars shimmer on the water and willed the tears back.

Tears she could keep from coming. She always had. The heartache she could not.

Back at home, Lukas wordlessly helped her from the boat.

They walked up the dock, stiff and distant. It was hard to believe that less than an hour ago they'd been as intimate as lovers.

'I must check on my father,' Lukas said when they came to the door. 'I've been gone too long as it is.' He gave a brusque nod of dismissal. 'I'll see you at dinner.'

'I'll eat in my room,' Rhiannon said, on an impulse born out of self-preservation. 'It's been a long day.'

'Hasn't it?' Lukas's smile was ironic. He touched the tip of his finger to her chin. 'You can't run from me for ever, Rhiannon. Remember what I said. I *will* have you.'

'We'll see about that,' she replied stiffly, and went to find Adeia and Annabel.

Annabel crowed with glee when she saw Rhiannon, her chubby arms outstretched. Rhiannon took her as a matter of course, smiled as she lay her downy head against her chest, arms curling around her neck.

'See how she loves you!' Adeia said with chuckling admiration. 'No baby could love her mama better.'

Rhiannon looked up in surprise. She hadn't realised how Annabel had begun to bond with her, or she with the baby. Her decision to stay had been one of the heart, yet it had been because of her own past rather than anything to do with Annabel.

She simply hadn't wanted any child to experience what she had.

Now, as Annabel snuggled against her, she realised she didn't want *this* child to experience it. This child—only this child—whom she loved.

She would do anything to keep her safe, secure. Loved.

Even marry Lukas?

Her thoughts were in a restless ferment as she fed Annabel in the kitchen, eating there as well, to make less work for Adeia.

Upstairs, she bathed the baby and gave her a bottle, her mind still whirling hopelessly.

Marrying Lukas would provide Annabel with a secure future. Lukas might not love her—might never love her—but he would certainly provide for her. She could trust him with her life, if not with her heart.

And a part of her, she knew, wanted to marry Lukas. Wanted to be with him…wanted to accept what little he gave because it was more than she'd ever had before.

Wanted to discover if that boy still existed underneath the man—if she could find him again, make him fall in love.

With her.

It was a recipe, Rhiannon thought, for disaster. For heartache.

Lukas stood quietly in the doorway, watching his father sleep. Regret and anger churned within him and he raked a hand through his hair in sheer annoyance.

He'd handled the outing with Rhiannon completely wrong. Worse, he'd put the proposal to her in exactly the way she would be sure to despise: as a matter of responsibility for both of them.

He should have played the besotted fool, pretended to be falling in love with her. She would have accepted that. He'd planned to take on the role when he'd put her on the boat, to set the stage for romance…seduction. Then his own sense of honour—not to mention dignity—had kept him from pretending to be something he wasn't. Something he never could be.

Yet to have put it so plainly, so coldly… Even he realised a woman like Rhiannon would rebel. Reject. He hadn't expected the swift, sudden stabbing pain when he'd heard her flat refusal. His pride had been hurt, but something else had as well. Something deeper.

He didn't like that realisation. Didn't like the thought that Rhiannon might be becoming important to him. Caring for someone was weakness. He knew that. He'd seen it.

He'd felt it.

Shaking his head, as if the brisk movement could banish the memories, the ghosts, the mocking laughter, Lukas turned his attention back to his father and saw the old man's eyes were open, watching him shrewdly.

'You look unhappy.'

'A bit annoyed, perhaps,' Lukas admitted in a clipped voice. 'Nothing that can't be set to rights. How are you, Papa?' He came into the room, his iron gaze sweeping the pitiful length of his father's diminished frame.

'I am as well as is to be expected,' Theo replied after a moment. His words were still slow, rasping. 'We knew this was going to happen.'

Lukas nodded—a choppy movement. Theo smiled. His eyes were tired. They'd lost a bit of their sharpness, their hardness, and now they looked at his son with a sorrow that thoroughly discomfited Lukas.

'You asked her to marry you?' Theo said finally. 'And she refused?'

'Yes.' Lukas didn't know how the old man knew so much, so well, but he accepted it with a shrug. 'As I told you.'

'Perhaps I should have told you how to go about wooing a woman,' Theo retorted, then shook his head, lying back against the pillows. 'You don't present it as a business contract, Lukas.'

'That's essentially what it is.'

'What you want it to be.' Theo lifted his head, looked at his son. 'Why can't you admit you care for her?'

'I've known her for less than a week,' Lukas snapped. 'I don't know why you've suddenly taken a fancy to believing life is like one of the old myths, but it is not. There are hard facts in place, and Rhiannon knows them as well as I do.'

Theo shook his head. 'No wonder she refused you.'

Again Lukas felt that stabbing pain, and hated it. He would not care. He would not. Yet he had told her he would have her, and he would.

'I expected as much,' he said irritably, and, swivelling on his heel, left the room.

The next morning, after a troubled, dreamless sleep, Rhiannon decided to check on Theo. He didn't need much care yet, as he spent most of his time sleeping or resting, but she took her responsibility seriously, light as it currently was.

She peeked into his bedroom after breakfast, and saw him looking alert and well rested.

'You look well.'

He smiled briefly. 'I feel well. For however long it lasts.'

'The doctor is coming back this afternoon to check on you.'

Theo shrugged. 'I don't need a doctor. We all know I'm going to die.'

'Yes,' Rhiannon agreed quietly, 'but there are still ways to go about it. To manage pain, increase comfort and dignity.'

Theo nodded, looking away. Understanding his need for a moment's silence, Rhiannon busied herself with refilling his water pitcher and straightening the bedcovers.

'Lukas cares for you,' Theo said after a moment. 'Though he'd descend to hell before admitting it.'

Rhiannon stiffened, straightened. 'Why are you telling me this?' she asked.

'Because I know he asked you to marry him, and I think it's the right thing to do.' It had taken Theo a while to say it, but his tone was still blunt.

'For Annabel?' Rhiannon stated flatly, and he nodded.

'Yes. And for you.'

'I won't be someone's responsibility.' Rhiannon shook his head. 'I'm sorry, Theo, because for whatever reasons you seem to want us to marry. Although I could've sworn you didn't like me when I arrived!'

Theo's smile glimmered briefly. 'I didn't, but then I saw how Lukas acted towards you. He has always told me he will never marry, and of course I want him to. I want grandsons even if I never see them. Heirs. And if he has in his heart chosen you—'

'He hasn't.' Rhiannon cut him off. 'And you already have a great-granddaughter who needs your love and affection. Lukas marrying me doesn't change that.'

Theo was silent for a moment. 'No,' he agreed, 'perhaps not.'

'I should go.' Her throat was tight, her mind seething once again.

Despite her firm refusals, there was a seed of hope, a spark of need, that had lodged itself under her ribs. She wanted to believe Lukas cared for her. She wanted to accept what little love she was given.

It was more than she'd ever had before, perhaps more than she'd ever be given.

A little.

Yet, Rhiannon wondered, could it ever be enough?

CHAPTER EIGHT

'THINGS have changed.'

Rhiannon looked up from where she was playing with Annabel on the sun-dappled floor of her bedroom. A shiver like an icy finger ran down her spine, despite the warmth of the room, the gurgle of Annabel's laughter.

'What are you talking about?' she asked, scooting off the floor so she could at least be almost at eye level with Lukas.

He stood before her, dressed in charcoal-grey trousers, belted narrowly at his hips, and a crisp white shirt open at the throat. His hair was newly washed and slicked back from his forehead, and his expression held foreboding. Anger. Resolution.

Nothing Rhiannon liked.

'Things have changed,' Lukas repeated, 'since we spoke yesterday. There are fewer choices.'

'Oh, really?' Rhiannon arched one eyebrow. 'Because it didn't seem like there were too many choices yesterday.'

'My lovely sister Antonia has got wind of what's going on. She wants Annabel.' He spoke flatly, harshly, and Rhiannon shook her head in confusion.

'Christos's mother? Annabel's grandmother?'

'Yes.'

'But…' Loss and fear were sweeping through her in empty consuming waves, yet she forced them back. 'Surely that's a good thing? You said Christos wasn't interested in Annabel, but if his mother is…'

'You don't know his mother.'

'But surely Annabel needs all the family she can have—' Rhiannon protested.

'Why? So you can make a quick escape? Changed your mind, Rhiannon?' Lukas jeered. 'Decided it's all too much for you? You want your life back? At least you can walk away.'

There was so much bitterness in his voice that Rhiannon could only shake her head in confusion. 'I'm not walking away,' she said finally. 'Even though at one point you wanted me to! But I'm not her mother, Lukas, even if I wanted to be, and I recognise who has the rights here.' She took a deep breath. 'I love Annabel. I realise that now. But she's not mine.' It hurt to say it—carved great, jagged pieces out of her soul—but she had to speak the truth. It was only what every newspaper, every judge, would say if it came to that.

'I thought you were different,' Lukas said after a moment, his voice flat. 'I thought you cared about Annabel and your responsibility to her.'

'And what *is* my responsibility?' Rhiannon flashed. 'To deny a child her family, her inheritance? Or to keep her all to myself simply because I want to? Because I want her? That's not duty, Lukas. It's desire. Sometimes,' she added icily, 'I think you confuse the two. It must make you feel better, to insist something you want is actually your responsibility. Does it relieve your guilt?'

There was a moment of silence so charged and appalling that Rhiannon felt as if she'd slapped him…hurt him. Lukas blinked, shook his head slowly.

'There may be some truth in what you say about a child's right to her family,' he said in a hard voice, 'but there's simply too much at stake. Antonia has rung me to say she wants custody—complete custody of Annabel. That means you wouldn't see her, I wouldn't see her, and she would grow up the plaything of a woman who's been a drug addict and a social parasite.'

His flat recitation of facts left Rhiannon chilled to the marrow.

'A judge would never grant custody to a woman like that,' she said after a moment, but her voice wavered.

'Wouldn't he? Antonia is the misunderstood darling of the newspapers. They report her antics and then spend pages explaining and forgiving her abominable behaviour. I blame myself; they need at least one Petrakides to give them news, and I don't. I never have.' He paused, and Rhiannon saw the guilt chase clearly across his features, reflected in the shadowy grey of his eyes, before it was replaced by the more familiar resolve.

'Antonia is Annabel's grandmother. I am only her great-uncle,' he continued tonelessly. 'In a court the judge is almost always going to side with a woman in custody cases—especially with one who bats her eyelashes and lets her lip tremble.' His own lip curled in a sneer. 'Antonia knows how to play people, and she'll play the judge. She'll parade witnesses to prove how she's changed her life, what a devoted mother she is.'

Rhiannon shook her head. 'But why? Surely she would only go to such lengths if she loved Annabel?'

'She's desperate.' Lukas cut across her. 'Antonia is unhappy, bored, and she's managed to convince herself that this is what she needs. If she can smear the Petrakides name while she's at it, all the better.'

Rhiannon shook her head, unable to take in the rapid change of circumstances.

'Surely she'd be willing to negotiate?' she said, a desperate edge entering her voice. 'Compromise…'

'Perhaps with me,' Lukas agreed coolly. 'But certainly not with you.'

Rhiannon blinked. It was the Petrakides family that had all the money, the power, the highly placed connections; she had to remember that.

'So what are you suggesting?' she finally asked, her voice a scratchy whisper.

'We get married. I know you didn't see the necessity of it before, but surely you do now? If we're married, providing Annabel with a stable home, and the judge knows that you've already forged a bond with her, Antonia's case will be weakened…perhaps so much that she'd be willing to drop the whole thing. She doesn't actually want Annabel. She just thinks she does. If she got custody she'd have Annabel kitted out with nannies and boarding schools and never see her. No one would.' He paused, his mouth twisting in a bitter grimace. 'Or, worse, she'd spoil her like a pet poodle—the way she did with Christos. You see how *he's* turned out.'

'I haven't actually met him,' Rhiannon reminded him, a touch of acid in her tone, and Lukas shrugged.

'You don't want to. So, what is it to be? Give Annabel up or marry me?'

Rhiannon opened her mouth, but only a soundless laugh came out. She couldn't quite believe this was happening—that Lukas had given her such a drastic ultimatum so quickly.

'What about the paternity test? We should at least wait till then. A judge wouldn't even look at the case without one…'

Lukas tensed, then shrugged. 'Such a test will only confirm what we already know. Meanwhile Antonia will have gathered evidence, splashed tawdry headlines in the press. My family can do without those.'

'But—'

'Annabel has the look of a Petrakides,' Lukas continued in a final tone. 'And we know that Christos was with your friend Leanne, that he used my name. The dates match up. There's no escape.'

Escape. It made Rhiannon feel as if they were both being trapped…trapped into a marriage neither of them wanted.

But I want this.

The thought, the realisation, frightened her with its potency and its truth. She wanted to be with Lukas. She was halfway to falling in love with him, with the man she hoped—prayed—was underneath.

She just didn't want it to be like this.

'Surely there are other alternatives…?'

'Wait and see? By that time it will be too late. Rhiannon, I won't lie to you.' His tone softened, and he reached out to touch her, stroke her shoulders. 'I want to marry you for Annabel's sake—because I know my duty to a child of my blood. I won't let her be raised by a vain, selfish brat of a woman—I won't. And you shouldn't either. I know Annabel isn't yours, but she is yours in your heart, and she will grow to love you as a mother if she doesn't already—which I think she does.' He pulled her gently towards him, and Rhiannon found herself moving closer with reluctant, hesitant steps. 'As for us, we could have a good marriage. Children of our own, perhaps.' Her eyes widened, and he smiled. 'Why not? Why can there not be a little happiness for us?'

'But you don't love me,' Rhiannon said flatly.

'No, but I want you. You know I do.'

'And you'll have me?' She repeated his earlier words with a dry smile.

Lukas's eyes flashed silver as he acknowledged this truth. 'Yes. I desire you, and I will die before I hurt you. I will protect you, care for you, give you everything in my power.' He dropped his hands from her shoulders to spread them briefly in appeal. 'What more can you honestly ask for?'

Love. Need. Him needing her. It was so simple, so obvious, but so impossible to explain to a man like Lukas, who only saw what should be done, not what he wanted to be done. Or what she wanted.

Or even what she really needed.

She glanced down at Annabel. The baby met her gaze and reached up chubby arms in helpless demand. Up. Up into arms where she would be safe and cuddled and loved.

Choking back a nameless sound of despair, Rhiannon bent down and scooped the solid, warm bundle of baby into her arms. She pressed a kiss onto the top of Annabel's silky curls, dark and soft just like Lukas's.

She couldn't abandon this baby. She'd already made that decision, even though she had doubted herself at every turn, every twist in the strange path of fate that had brought her here.

Yet now she wondered if this opportunity was heaven-sent— given to her as a second chance. A chance to show a little girl how she could be loved. Loved by someone who had not given birth to her but who had chosen to be her mother. A mother who would never shirk her responsibility because that duty was not dreaded but desired, joyfully carried out.

She looked up, saw the flickering of warmth in Lukas's steady gaze—and saw something deeper as well.

I want him.

She would take a little. Even if it wasn't what she'd once dreamed of. Even if he didn't love her. Even if that knowledge seared her, stabbed her, hurt her more than she wanted to acknowledge, more than she wanted to feel.

She'd do it for Annabel and, she knew, because she wanted to. No matter how much it hurt.

She'd do it because this was Lukas.

'All right,' she whispered, and trembled inwardly at Lukas's smile of pure, primal victory.

The next few days passed in a blur of activity. Lukas was everywhere—on the telephone, on the internet, in the helicopter—arranging the small wedding that would be held on the island. Theo was exultant, and although his health was still failing there was a bloom in his cheeks, a sparkle in his eyes. He was a happy and triumphant man.

Rhiannon was numb. She cared for Annabel, she listened to the plans and conversations whirling around and above her, but found she could not consider what she'd done, what was happening.

What her future looked like.

When Lukas asked if there was anyone from Wales she'd like to invite to the wedding she merely shook her head. She found she wanted to be alone, away from the hive of expectant enterprise the villa had become.

Leaving Adeia in charge of Annabel, she escaped to the beach, walked along the silken sands, let the warm Aegean waters lap over her feet and soothe her soul.

What have I done?

She pressed her cold hands to her cheeks, closed her eyes.

Only what I needed to.
Only what I wanted to.

She could be happy with Lukas. She could let herself be happy. She knew he was only marrying her for Annabel, knew he didn't love her, no matter the desire—the lust—that pulsed between them.

It was still more than she'd ever had before.

She came to the rocky outcropping that separated the villa's beach from the private one she and Lukas had visited, and after a moment's pause she scrambled over the sharp rocks, picking her way carefully along the top till the hidden beach—Lukas's beach—their beach—came into view. As she made her way down she slipped, slicing her shin open on a jagged rock.

Muttering a curse under her breath, Rhiannon slid to the sand, covered the scrape with her hand. Blood trickled out between her fingers. She drew her knees up to her chest, laid her head against them, and wept.

The tears she'd held in since this whole crazy episode had begun came out in a hot, furious rush, a desperately needed release. There was no one to hear, no one to censure, no one to tell her to stop the theatrics, as her parents always had.

She hadn't cried like this in years, a numb, detached part of her brain acknowledged, even as the sobs came out—noisy, gulping ones, inelegant, ugly. Her face was wet, splotched, flushed.

She wiped her cheeks with the backs of her hands, thinking she was done, but the tears kept coming.

She had so many tears. Tears for the girl she'd been, lost and confused and begging for love, and tears for the woman she'd become, alone, afraid, seeking to love and be loved. She wouldn't beg any more, but she still wanted the happy ending.

The fairy tale that Lukas now demanded she relinquish for real life, hard facts.

'Rhiannon!'

Rhiannon looked up, saw Lukas towering above her on the rocks like a dark angel. He climbed nimbly down, his face drawn in lines of tender anxiety.

'Rhiannon, I've been looking for you. I heard the noises—I thought it was a hurt animal. What is wrong?'

'Nothing,' she denied, and he looked incredulous.

'You are crying as if your heart has been broken and you tell me nothing is wrong? I'm to be your husband. You must confide in me.'

'I must?' she repeated with a broken little laugh. She found she didn't care how ridiculous or pathetic she looked. It had felt good to cry.

'Rhiannon. Please. I want to know.' He took her hands in his, glanced down and exclaimed at the bloody cut on her leg. 'What happened? Is this why you are crying?' He looked up at her face, assessing, swift. 'But, no. It is something else. Still...' He withdrew a handkerchief from his pocket and pressed it to the cut. 'You must let Adeia see to it when you return to the villa.'

'I'll see to it myself,' Rhiannon protested, and he shrugged.

'As you wish. It is a nasty cut. Now...' He let his fingers cup her cheek, but Rhiannon didn't lean into that gentle caress—wouldn't let herself. Lukas noticed; she saw the flash of acknowledgement in his eyes. 'What is wrong?'

'Everything. Nothing.'

He shook his head, curbing his impatience. 'Tell me.'

She jerked her chin from his hand and looked out at the flat, calm surface of the sea. 'Lukas, my whole life has changed in a matter of days. I've agreed to marry a man I barely know, a man who has told me quite clearly he doesn't love me and won't ever love me. I know you think this is only what I should be doing, what it's my responsibility to do, and perhaps you're right. God knows, I've lived my whole life doing what I should do, what people expected me to do, no matter how much it hurt. But I thought...' She drew in a shaky breath, let it out in a rush. 'I thought, when my parents died, that part of my life was over. I thought that maybe, just maybe, I could start living for myself. That sounds terribly selfish, doesn't it? But I didn't mean it that way. I just wanted a little pleasure, a little fun...a little love.'

'And you think you're sacrificing all those by marrying me?' Lukas asked quietly.

'The love—certainly. You've said as much. Pleasure?' She glanced at him, managed a wry smile. 'I'm sure we'll find some pleasure. As for fun... You don't seem like a fun guy.'

'No?' He sat next to her, trailed his fingers thoughtfully in the sand. 'No, I don't suppose there's been much time for fun in my life. I always do what I'm supposed to as well. What is expected...what I expect of myself.'

'And now—this marriage—isn't it just more of the same?' Rhiannon asked, knowing the answer and yet wanting it to be different. Wanting Lukas to tell her that, no, this was not about duty. This was about what he wanted. Wanting to believe the fairy tale even now.

'It is a duty,' Lukas said after a moment. 'But that doesn't mean it has to become a burden. We can be a family for Annabel, for each other. It can be good.'

Rhiannon nodded. Good. She'd wanted something great. Something big and magical and wonderful. But she'd settle for good. She'd make herself.

'Come back to the house,' Lukas urged gently. 'See to your cut and have dinner. The arrangements have been made. I was coming to tell you. We can marry tomorrow.'

Rhiannon's head jerked up. 'Tomorrow?'

'I thought the sooner the better,' Lukas admitted. 'Selfish, perhaps. But I want you, Rhiannon. Soon. I want you tomorrow.'

'Who is coming?'

'No one who isn't already here. We can have a reception in Athens later, if you like. You can meet my colleagues, as well as other members of the family. Invite friends from Wales.'

'I told you, there is no one.'

'No one?'

Rhiannon shrugged. Her handful of casual friends had never become more than acquaintances. She'd spent so long on her own, nursing her parents, that she'd forgotten how to socialise, how to be fun and light and chatty. If she'd ever known how.

She'd dated a few men—co-workers who had dropped her when she hadn't been bubbly, engaging, or free enough with her favours, and Rhiannon hadn't even minded.

That life had been small, cold. Hopeless. It had been hers, yet she hadn't realised until now just how pathetically empty it had been.

Perhaps that was in part why it had been so easy in the end to agree.

'Theo and Adeia will be witnesses,' Lukas said, 'and the priest from Naxos will fly in to marry us. I didn't think you'd mind something small.'

'I don't,' Rhiannon admitted. 'It's just all so sudden.'

'Let yourself go,' Lukas urged, and the warm caress of his words reminded her of a far more intimate encounter they'd shared not too far from here. She could almost feel his fingers on her, in her.

'I suppose I have no choice,' she said, trying to sound light and sounding brittle instead. She shrugged and stood up, brushing the damp sand from her shorts.

Lukas watched her for a moment, eyes dark, guarded, thoughtful.

'You have choices,' he said after a moment. He was still sitting, looking up at her with knowing eyes. 'You could walk away. Walk away from me now. I'd let you.'

Rhiannon stared at him, saw the dark hunger in his eyes. He was testing her, and perhaps himself. He sat completely still. Tense, watching.

'I'm not walking away from anyone now,' she said quietly. 'I've made my decision, Lukas. I'll stand by it.'

She was surprised at the naked relief on his face before it was masked. 'Good.'

He stood up, took her hand, and led her carefully back over the rocks.

The day of her wedding dawned pearly and fresh, with a warm, promising breeze rolling off the sea. Rhiannon stood at the window, breathing in the fresh, salty air, letting it fill her. Fill her with hope.

She didn't want to start her wedding day—her marriage—with bitterness and recrimination. She'd cried all her tears yesterday. There would be none today.

Today was for beginnings, for beauty. For the possibility of what could be, limited as it sometimes seemed.

She looked through her clothes for an appropriate wedding dress—Lukas hadn't seemed to remember that little detail in all of his planning. There was nothing remotely bridal, and she was choosing between the little yellow sundress and the loose silk trousers when a knock sounded at the door.

'Come in.'

It was Adeia, smiling shyly and holding a hanger swathed in plastic. 'Master Lukas—he doesn't think of everything,' she said in careful English. 'Not as much as he thinks he does. He forgot your dress, no?'

'He did,' Rhiannon admitted with a rueful laugh, and Adeia thrust the swathed hanger forward.

'For you.'

Rhiannon took it in surprise. 'But how…?'

Adeia pointed to her chest. 'Mine.'

'Your dress?' Rhiannon asked, hoping her scepticism did not show on her face. Adeia had to be sixty years old at least, and she was stout and round. Never mind the style or condition of the dress, Rhiannon couldn't imagine it would fit her.

'I make some changes,' Adeia said with a little grin. 'You see.'

Carefully Rhiannon took the plastic off, and gasped at the dress that lay beneath. It was a traditional Greek outfit, with a white linen under-dress, and sleeves decorated with brightly coloured embroidered bands. A scarlet apron sewn with gold coins was there to go over the dress.

'It's beautiful, Adeia,' Rhiannon said. 'Like something out of a story!'

'You'll wear it?'

'Absolutely. Thank you for lending it to me.'

Adeia beamed, and Rhiannon kissed her weathered cheek.

It didn't take long to slip on the dress and apron, and Rhiannon was amazed at the transformation. With her olive colouring and dark, curly hair she could pass for Greek anyway, and now, with the dress, she felt as wild and free as a peasant girl.

She didn't look like someone who was afraid or desperate— someone who cared what people thought of her. In this dress she could be anyone she wanted to be. She could be a woman who laughed and grabbed at life with both hands...who took what was offered and enjoyed it.

That was who she wanted to be.

That was who she *would* be.

She kept her feet and head bare, and went in search of the wedding party...and her groom.

The wedding was to be held on the beach, and as tradition demanded Lukas was waiting with her bouquet at the front door.

'Everyone is ready and waiting outside,' he said softly as she came down the stairs. 'The priest is here.' He let out a low, delighted chuckle as he surveyed her costume. 'Who is this Greek princess coming to visit me?'

Rhiannon smiled. 'Do you like it?'

'Very much.' He handed her the flowers, a simple bouquet of wild orchids tied with ribbon.

Rhiannon knew the wedding ceremony would be traditional Greek Orthodox, as Lukas had requested, and now she found herself wondering just what it would be like.

Lukas took her arm and they walked together down to the beach. The sun was high and bright in the sky, the only sound the gentle lapping of the sea on sand.

Theo, Adeia with Annabel in her arms, her husband Athos, and the priest, a smiling, bearded man in his thirties, all waited at the beach. Everyone beamed when they saw her, delighted by her dress, and perhaps by the simple fact that a wedding was taking place.

Lukas Petrakides was getting married. Without pomp or paparazzi, or any fuss at all.

It amazed her, stunned her that this was happening—that she was entering this world...Lukas's world.

Rhiannon didn't understand much of the Greek that was spoken, although she understood the symbolism. The priest blessed the two rings Lukas had procured, and placed them in their hands.

Rhiannon watched the burnished gold band slide onto her finger, felt the strange, heavy weight of it.

Theo swapped the rings between Lukas and Rhiannon three times, much to her bemusement. Lukas grinned and whispered, 'It's tradition. You'll find we do many things three times.'

Was she imagining the lascivious intent in those words?

The priest joined their hands, and Rhiannon felt a bolt of awareness travel from her fingers to her toes, straight through her heart, at the feel of Lukas's warm, dry hand encasing hers.

After some prayers, the priest brandished two flowered crowns and laid them on her and Lukas's heads.

'The *stefana*,' Lukas explained in a murmur. 'They symbolise the glory and honour we have received.'

Glory. Honour. Lofty words for a marriage that was simply a matter of necessity.

Rhiannon smiled in understanding, but she wasn't sure she really understood.

Everything felt so special, so romantic. So sacred. And yet it wasn't exactly real…was it?

Theo exchanged the crowns between them three times, and Rhiannon met Lukas's laughing gaze with a smile of her own.

Then the priest proffered a cup of wine, and Lukas told her they must each drink from it three times.

The priest took their hands and led them around the makeshift altar. Rhiannon followed, bemused when he broke the ribbon that had joined their crowns and, with a wide smile, pronounced them man and wife.

'Married,' Lukas murmured, and there was blatant satisfaction—possession—in his voice.

Married. For better, for worse. For ever.

She just hoped they'd done the right thing. For Annabel…and for themselves.

Adeia had prepared a wedding breakfast in the villa, and they all retired there for the celebration.

Rhiannon found she enjoyed the simple food and conversation. Simple pleasures. Easy. Enjoyment that postponed what she knew would come—what she both dreaded and desired.

'You should go,' Theo chided when the meal was long-finished and they were still sitting among the scattered remains. 'The boat ride is at least an hour.'

'Boat ride?'

Theo pretended to look abashed, and Lukas rolled his eyes. 'Yes, boat ride. We have to go somewhere for our honeymoon, don't we?'

Rhiannon shrugged. 'Do we?' They were already on a magnificent island—where else could they go?

'We do,' he replied firmly. 'Adeia has seen to your bags. All you need do is change, and we will be off.'

Rhiannon felt the first stirrings of genuine excitement. She hadn't been off the island in over a week, and the quarters, although luxurious, could sometimes be cramped. She realised she was looking forward to going somewhere new...with Lukas.

It was late afternoon before they were actually aboard Lukas's boat, with baggage stowed, ready to sail.

Theo and Adeia saw them off, and even Annabel waved from the housekeeper's comfortable embrace.

'She'll be all right,' Lukas said quietly, clearly reading Rhiannon's thoughts. 'It's only for one night.'

She nodded agreement, though she was reluctant to relinquish her care of Annabel even for so short a time. The little girl had barely been out of her sight since Leanne had died.

'So, where are we going?'

Lukas, dressed in faded chinos and a blue cotton shirt open at the neck, smiled mischievously over one shoulder as he hoisted the sail. 'You've been on a private and secluded island already, so I thought to myself, What else can I give you? And then the answer came.' He paused, eyes dancing, and Rhiannon laughed.

'What?'

'Company.'

Still mystified, she shook her head, and Lukas smiled. 'You'll see.'

The sun had started to sink towards the waves when the boat finally approached land. There was a neat cove, twinkling with lights, framed by whitewashed buildings with brightly painted doors and shutters.

'Amorgos—the nearest island,' Lukas explained. 'A small place, as yet mostly undiscovered by tourists.'

'You don't want to build the next Petra Resort here?' Rhiannon teased, and he pretended to shudder.

'No, never.' He moored the boat by one of the docks, and helped her out onto the weathered wood.

'You look beautiful,' he murmured as she took his hand. 'I bought that dress hoping I'd one day see you in it.'

'You saw me in it the other day,' Rhiannon protested. She looked down at the short, flirty sundress, its simple fabric skimming over her body, hinting at the curves underneath.

'Yes…but this is how I imagined it. You, here, belonging to me.' His hands touched her waist gently, and he brushed her mouth in the lightest of kisses—a promise, Rhiannon knew, of what was ahead.

Fear and anticipation unfurled in equal amounts in her middle, spread grasping tendrils throughout her limbs, so her only response was a slight shake of her head.

'Lukas…'

'We can talk later,' he promised softly. 'Now we eat. And dance. And sing!'

Laughing, Rhiannon let him pull her along, down the dock, into the music and lights of the village.

They walked down a cobbled street to a taverna whose tables stretched right to the water. There was little more than a lapping sound as fishing boats gently nudged each other in the darkness.

The taverna was crowded with people, most of whom seemed to know Lukas and called to him with joyful, unaffected greetings. Lukas responded in kind, with laughter and slaps on the back, while Rhiannon watched, bemused. She felt as if she were seeing a different Lukas—one she hadn't believed existed.

No one here cared that Lukas ran a real estate empire. No one bowed and scraped. Here they were all friends, and the older men treated him like a younger brother, or a son, despite the fact that he could most likely buy the entire island twice over with his pocket change.

Lukas, his arm around her shoulders, drew Rhiannon into the crowd and lights. Rhiannon heard him speak Greek, and knew he was introducing her as his wife simply by the way jaws dropped and eyes widened—before the night descended into a cacophony of congratulations.

When they were seated at a table, with large glasses of rich red wine set in front of them, as well as a dish of olives, Rhiannon raised her eyebrows.

'You're known here?'

Lukas shrugged, smiled. 'I'm known everywhere.'

Rhiannon shook her head slightly at the inherent arrogance in the simple statement. That was the Lukas she knew, understood. Yet she also knew she was seeing a different Lukas now—a man who was more human and perhaps more like her than she'd ever dared imagine.

'Yes,' she said, 'but everywhere you're known as Lukas Petrakides, reclusive real estate tycoon. Here you're known simply as yourself…aren't you?'

He gazed at her, his eyes turning silver in the moonlight, a thoughtful expression on his face. 'Yes…perhaps you're right. Here I am myself. My grandmother was from Amorgos before she moved to Athens in search of work. When my father bought our island I spent many of my boyhood days here. Happy days.'

In an otherwise unhappy existence? Rhiannon wanted to ask, but didn't. Slowly she was gaining a picture of Lukas's life…of a childhood torn apart by a mother who followed her lover rather than her family, a father who instilled in him an unshakable, crippling sense of his own responsibility.

'What made you happy?' she asked, and Lukas shrugged.

'Simple boyhood things. Fishing, swimming, learning to sail.'

'With people who loved you?' It slipped out before she could help it, and Rhiannon bit her lip. She didn't want to start an argument. She didn't want to hear his cold denial.

There was a moment of silence, and in the flickering lights Rhiannon couldn't see the expression on Lukas's face as he toyed with his wine glass.

'Yes,' he said at last. 'There is something in that.'

Her heart bumped against her ribs as she realised what he was saying.

The boy underneath the man. Still there.

'Our childhoods were similar in some ways,' she said, 'despite the obvious differences.'

He raised his eyebrows in silent question.

'You had a lot more money,' Rhiannon hastened to explain, 'yet at the same time we were both—' She stopped, unsure if she should continue with the bleak picture she was painting.

'Both…?' Lukas prompted.

'Unhappy,' she finished softly, and looked down at her drink.

'Good thing we have both learned to be happy,' Lukas finally said, and there was a flat neutrality to his voice that told Rhiannon the moment of intimacy—of connection—was over.

'They didn't know you were married,' she observed after a moment, and Lukas chuckled.

'No one does. Right now it's a well-kept secret.'

'The press will go wild, I suppose,' she said gloomily, and Lukas covered her hand with his own.

'That is why I married you—to shield you from such specu- lation. They *will* go wild, but it will die down. If you hadn't married me, Rhiannon, they would have written that you were my mistress, or worse.' He shook his head. 'I did not want that.'

'No.' Rhiannon tried to ignore the leaden feeling his words had caused. *That is why I married you.* One of the many cool, practical reasons. 'How did you know all these friends would be here if you didn't tell them?' she asked.

'I have my ways.' Lukas's smile was a flash of white in the oncoming twilight. 'I told them I had a surprise to show them tonight. But they never would have thought of a wife!'

'It seems that no one ever thought you'd get married at all.'

'I always said I wouldn't,' Lukas admitted with a tiny shrug.

'Why not? Surely your responsibility includes providing a Petrakides heir?'

Lukas was silent for a moment, his face hard, and Rhiannon wondered if she'd pressed, pushed, too hard. It was a simple question, yet she was aware of the subtle jibe underneath.

'I have three sisters to provide heirs,' Lukas finally dismissed. 'And my sense of responsibility only extends so far.'

Rhiannon's eyes widened. Was Lukas actually saying that there was something he *wouldn't* do out of duty? Marry? Yet that was exactly what he'd done.

'I've really slipped the noose around your neck, haven't I?' she joked feebly, hearing the horrible, hollow sound of her voice.

'No. It was my idea, my choice. And it is no noose, Rhiannon, unless we choose to make it so.'

Rhiannon heard the warning and heeded it. It would take two to make this marriage work. She understood that. She only hoped they would both be able to hold up their end of this awkward bargain.

A red-faced man with a curly beard approached the table, clapping his hands and urging Lukas and Rhiannon to rise.

'They want us to dance,' Lukas explained with a little smile. 'The Syrtos—a traditional Greek wedding dance.'

'I don't know the steps,' she protested, even as he pulled her to her feet.

'You'll figure it out.' He wrapped his arm around her shoulder, pressing her to his side. Rhiannon could feel the warm, steady heat of him all along her body, felt her own blood pulse and heat in response.

Musicians were playing a merry if somewhat discordant tune, and everyone had gathered into a circle, arms around each other's shoulders, stamping their feet and shouting.

Rhiannon was pulled into the circle, pressed next to Lukas, and then they began to move.

It was a simple rotation of steps—right foot, back, left foot—but Rhiannon soon found it hardly mattered what foot she put where. Everyone was moving as they wanted to, stamping and leaping and roaring with laughter.

Somehow, somewhere, she let her inhibitions slip away and reminded herself of that wild peasant girl who'd looked back from the mirror that morning. A girl who didn't cling or beg for love. A girl who was wild and free. For a few moments, with the music and the laughter and the lights, she became that girl.

The night passed in a whirl of colour and sound, of food and drink, and embraces and smacking kisses on both cheeks. Rhiannon barely understood most of what was said, but it didn't matter. She certainly got the gist.

The moonlight was turning the sea to silver by the time Lukas finally said they had to depart—news which was greeted with cheers and ribald laughter.

Shaking his finger warningly at the crowd, yet chuckling a bit too, he led Rhiannon down the cobbled street.

'Some of them have had too much to drink,' Lukas said in half-apology, but Rhiannon, who was feeling pleasantly dozy from three glasses of wine, just giggled.

'I don't mind.'

'They mean well.'

'I gathered that…though I barely understood a word that was said!' She laughed, and it turned into a hiccup.

Lukas stopped, his hands on her shoulders, and turned her to face him.

'Rhiannon, you're not drunk, are you?' His lips were twitching, eyes sparkling, yet he still managed to look serious.

Rhiannon looked indignant. 'Drunk? Hardly! I had a few glasses of wine!'

'It's strong stuff.'

'I'm fine.' She tried to shrug away, but Lukas steadied her with one finger on her chin.

'Good,' he breathed, drawing her lips closer to his own, 'because I don't want you out of your head on our wedding night…in our wedding bed.'

'I'm—' His lips touched her own. A brief caress, nothing more. Yet it flickered awareness straight to Rhiannon's soul, acted like a bucket of icy water drenching her nerves, making her stone-cold sober and yet gloriously alive. 'Not,' she finished in a whisper, hearing the breathiness of her voice, seeing Lukas's knowing smile.

'Good. Our hotel is just this way.' He led her down the street, past quaint shops shuttered for the night, to a simple courtyard with high white walls and an iron gate, its interior filled with pots of geraniums and bougainvillaea. 'It's a simple place,' Lukas warned her. 'There are no luxurious resorts on Amorgos. But I think it will suit our needs.'

Rhiannon merely nodded. For the reality of their situation was becoming very much present, and her heart was beginning to thrum in heady response.

Lukas fished a key out of his pocket and opened the door. Their bags had already been placed inside the room, which was simple, yet clean and welcoming.

A wide pine bed with white linen sheets dominated the space. A large window above it looked out onto the harbour, its sashes thrown wide open. A slightly battered dresser was across from the bed, and a door led to a bathroom.

Rhiannon loved it. She didn't want luxury, didn't want more examples of Lukas's wealth and power. She wanted this…a simple, clean room and the two of them.

Lukas cleared his throat, and Rhiannon wondered if he felt some of the awkwardness she was experiencing.

'Would you like a bath?'

'I'll clean up a bit,' she said, brushing back her tangled curls with a self-conscious hand.

Lukas gestured to the bathroom, and Rhiannon spent a few awkward seconds scrambling in her bag for her nightgown while he stretched out on the bed, calm and relaxed.

Her fist closed around the filmy scrap of material, the night-gown he'd purchased for her only a week ago—although he could have hardly had *this* scenario in mind. Could he?

'I'll be right back,' she mumbled, and bolted into the bathroom.

She didn't want a bath. Only a few moments to calm her racing heart and figure out a way to approach this…situation.

Rhiannon's mouth twisted in a wry smile. The situation, she acknowledged, was sex, pure and simple. Something she'd never done before. She didn't know if Lukas knew that, or had simply guessed it. Wasn't sure she should say.

Twenty-six-year-old women were rarely virgins these days, she knew. Although she suspected Lukas would have an irritatingly arrogant satisfaction in learning that he was her first, her only lover, Rhiannon felt encumbered by her lack of experience.

She glanced in the mirror, saw her flushed face, bright eyes, the wild tangle of hair. She still looked like that peasant girl.

If only she could be like that now…confident, in control. For so much of her life she'd let other people dictate who she was, what she did—and all to get the smallest scrap of affection. Of love.

She didn't want to be that way with Lukas. She refused to live in his shadow, to beg for love she knew he wasn't willing to give. Yet she also recognised her own helpless, hopeless tendency to do just that.

She slipped off the sundress, reached for the virginal white nightgown—something that spoke of bridal sacrifice. Then she stopped.

She wouldn't be that girl. She would be a woman—full, free. That was how she wanted to start this marriage. That was how she would go on.

Taking a deep breath, she opened the bathroom door.

Lukas glanced up when she opened the door, his eyes flaring in admiring surprise when he saw what she wore: nothing.

Rhiannon stood there, shoulders thrown back proudly, eyes blazing challenge. 'I'm ready.'

'I'd say so,' Lukas murmured, swinging his legs off the bed. His hands went to the buttons of his shirt. 'I think *I* need to be ready…'

'No.' Rhiannon strode forward, stilled his hands with her own. 'Let me.'

Lukas hesitated, his gaze sweeping the naked length of her, and part of Rhiannon—a large part—wanted to cover herself. Hide.

Yet she didn't. Lukas acquiesced, leaned back against the pillow. Smiling a little at this victory, Rhiannon began unbuttoning his shirt.

Her fingers trembled a tiny bit as she worked the buttons through the cloth, exposing a broad expanse of perfect bronzed flesh. She smoothed her hands across his bare chest, smiling as Lukas shuddered slightly in response.

She pulled the shirt off his shoulders and he helped her by shrugging it to the floor. Then her hands went to his belt buckle—and stopped.

Lukas was still, silent, waiting for her lead.

After a moment Rhiannon undid the belt, slipped it through the loops and tossed it to the floor. She unbuttoned his trousers, tugged at the zip while her knuckles brushed his straining hardness.

She began to pull off his trousers, her hands skimming down his legs, while Lukas suppressed an oath and kicked them off.

'I'm finding it hard to wait,' he muttered thickly, and at the blatant look of desire hazing his eyes Rhiannon felt her own response leap to life, race through her veins, fill her with heady power.

'You'll have to wait a little longer,' she said, an ancient, womanly smile curving her lips.

Lukas groaned and leaned back against the pillows. An offering to her. Hers.

He still wore his boxer briefs, yet Rhiannon didn't hesitate as she reached for them—for him. Now she wanted to see him. She felt her own power, felt the excitement and passion coursing between them, and it urged her on.

The briefs fell to the floor and Lukas lay there, naked, magnificent. Rhiannon's breath caught in her lungs at the sight of him.

She reached a hand out, curled it around him, heard his choked moan as she stroked him softly.

'Rhiannon…let me touch you…'

'Soon,' she promised, and laughed deep in her throat at Lukas's moan of pleasure. 'I've never been touched before, you know,' she said softly. 'Did you know that? Did you know I've never had a lover?'

'I wondered,' he choked out as her hand continued its bold stroking. 'Although it's rather difficult to believe right now…'

'Is it?' she murmured. Her fingers drifted up his chest, teased his nipples. She leaned over him, her breasts skimming his chest, and kissed him deeply.

Lukas returned the kiss, his hands coming to her shoulders. 'Let me touch you,' he whispered, and she did.

She took his hands, drew them to her breasts. Now she was the one giving in to pleasure, moaning in delight and awe as his hands caressed her, his fingers teasing her with knowing assurance, before he bent his head and applied his mouth to where his hands had been.

Her own hands fisted in his hair, pulled her to him in silent demand.

He stretched out beside her, his hands skimming her skin, teasing the juncture of her thighs. 'It's been a long time for me,' he admitted, his voice hoarse, 'but I don't want to rush you.' He paused. 'I don't want to hurt you.'

'You won't,' Rhiannon said, amazed at her own confidence, her audacity. She drew his hand back to her legs. 'Touch me.'

And he did, his fingers slipping inside, his eyes burning into hers.

'You're beautiful…' he whispered, and she *felt* beautiful.

She'd shed her fear like a tired skin. She felt new and strong and powerful. She gasped as his fingers continued to stroke her into flames, a whirling torrent of need and pleasure that overwhelmed her, caused her to gasp and cry out.

'Lukas…'

'Let yourself go,' he commanded, and she laughed shakily, pulling him towards her in an urgent kiss.

'I *am*…'

'Good.'

She was so close to the edge, to explosion. Her hips moved restlessly, rhythmically, seeking the release she knew would come.

Yet she didn't want it to be like this, with Lukas in control, his eyes glazed with desire.

'*You* let yourself go,' she demanded, and his eyes widened as she rolled on top of him and began to draw him into her own warmth.

It was a strange new feeling, this filling inside her, yet it was welcome. She laughed aloud as Lukas gasped and began to move, clasping her hips to his.

'Am I hurting you?' he asked raggedly, and she laughed again. The twinge of pain had been lost in the haze of feeling—wonderful, glorious, hot.

'No,' she said, 'you're not hurting me.'

Then they were both lost to the rhythmic movement, this ancient dance. Rhiannon didn't need to be taught, didn't need to be shown. She knew. She felt him deep inside her, could see how their bodies were joined as one.

It was wondrous. It was beautiful.

It was love.

She gave herself up to the exquisite sensation, allowed herself to be fully possessed. Consumed. She heard Lukas cry out, heard their voices joining as their bodies were joined, and knew she loved him.

Loved him.

She also knew—realised it with an intense, wonderful rush—that love didn't make you weak. It made you vulnerable, but it also made you strong.

She loved him.

The thought didn't humble her, didn't frighten her. It only made her smile. It made her cry out when release came, hot and joyous and fast, and she smoothed Lukas's hair back with gentle fingers as he buried his face in her neck, his own breath choked and ragged.

I love you. She wanted to say it. Opened her mouth to. Yet breathed the words back in before they were more than a whisper of sound.

He didn't want to hear that. Would be appalled, horrified. Perhaps even angry.

Lukas didn't understand about love, Rhiannon realised with a rush of sweet sorrow. He only saw it as weakness, causing hurt, pain, problems.

Yet once he'd loved. Needed love, wanted it. The boy underneath. She would find him. She could.

She would have to.

CHAPTER NINE

'WHAT shall we do today?'

Lukas was lying next to her, his head propped on one hand, as the early-morning sun dappled the floor in dusty beams and the sea sparkled outside like a jewel.

Rhiannon felt a warm glow spread through her, as if she'd swallowed sunshine, and the sum of her lonely, loveless years melted to nothing as she basked in the easy affection of Lukas's gaze.

She smiled up at him, shrugging. 'Anything.'

'Anything?' Lukas repeated, trailing one tempting finger along her bare ribcage.

'Anything,' Rhiannon agreed, even as desire began to flow through her, turning her both weak and strong. She wanted his touch, and was unafraid to show it.

Lukas kissed her, his hands stroking her body to flame, and Rhiannon gave herself up to the glorious sensation of being loved.

Loved.

She wanted to believe it—wanted to believe that Lukas could love her. That perhaps he did love her, even if he refused to acknowledge it.

Was she completely naive? She pushed the thought away.

Afterwards as they lay together, Lukas's fingers absently stroking circles on her midriff, Rhiannon felt compelled to say, 'I don't want to leave Annabel for too long.'

'No,' Lukas agreed. 'We can sail back this afternoon. But this morning...'

'Is half gone,' Rhiannon finished ruefully, for the sun that shone on them now was hot and high in the sky.

'We can have breakfast in Katapola,' Lukas decided, 'and perhaps visit the ruins. There's an ancient village near here, but everyone was forced to flee when a fire destroyed most of the trees and livestock. It turned Amorgos to a barren, lifeless island for hundreds of years.'

'But it's come back to life now?' Rhiannon said with a little smile, and she couldn't ignore the similar question unfurling in her own heart: could it happen to Lukas?

Could she breathe life into his loveless existence? Resurrect his faith in love?

She didn't know. Hers had been, but she'd been hungry for it. Ready to believe. Ready to love.

Lukas wasn't.

Still, she wanted to believe it could happen—and that she could be the one to do it.

After they'd dressed, they breakfasted at a café by the harbour, eating yoghurt and honey and drinking strong coffee.

At a market stall Lukas bought bottled water and a straw hat for Rhiannon, for their dusty walk into the hills.

They left the lively village streets behind them for a dirt track that wound its way through rocky fields, up into the hills that Rhiannon saw were scattered with ruined stone—the crumbling foundations of an ancient town, an ancient life.

The only sound was a distant goat's bell, and the rustle of grass as they walked. She could smell the clean, dry scent of wild rosemary and thyme, mingled with the tang of salt from the sea.

'Have no archaeologists come to investigate all this?' she asked, as Lukas showed her the half-standing walls of what looked to be a potter's house.

He shrugged. 'Amorgos likes to keep things the way they are. There are so many ruins in Greece—a few untouched ones will hardly go amiss.'

'It's nice that it's left like this,' Rhiannon agreed, and he nodded. 'No one to spoil it.'

He linked his hand with hers—a careless, affectionate gesture that still managed to go straight to her heart.

'You're like a different man here,' she said impulsively. 'Not the real estate tycoon.'

'Tycoon?' He laughed dryly. 'Is that how you see me?'

'That's how the world sees you. Intimidating, remote, powerful. Do you know how scared I was when I first sought you out in that bar?'

'Were you?' Lukas murmured, and suddenly Rhiannon remembered that sizzling moment of connection, the way she'd been drawn to him as if pulled by a wire.

'I want us to be like this,' she confessed softly.

Lukas turned to her, his eyes dark, questioning. 'Like what, Rhiannon?'

If there was a challenge in his voice, she didn't heed it. Didn't want to. 'Happy.'

He nodded. 'I would like us to be happy too,' he said, his face averted, and already Rhiannon felt as if she were losing him, as if he were pulling away.

They were both silent. The dry grass tickled Rhiannon's bare legs as she sat on an old block of stone, the last remnant of someone's house, someone's life.

The sun beat down hotly and the sky was a bright, hard blue, without a cloud in sight. The sea was a flat mirror, reflecting the brilliant sunshine.

The moment, the easy intimacy, was slipping away, and Rhiannon didn't want it to go. Wouldn't let it.

'What if things change?' she asked, quietly enough that Lukas might not have heard her. Her heart was pounding and her mouth was dry, but she had to know.

Lukas heard, and he swivelled to face her, eyes alert with wary challenge. 'What might change?'

'What if...?' She licked her lips, continued. 'What if we fell in love...with each other?'

The silence was awful, terrifying in its blank rejection. Rhiannon stared down at her feet, her toes curling inwards as her whole body wanted to hide from the question she'd put out there so baldly, so boldly, when she didn't really have the courage to see it through.

She saw Lukas's feet move, felt him crouch next to her.

'Rhiannon.'

His fingers were on her chin, lifting her face to meet his own unyielding gaze.

'Rhiannon,' he repeated, in a voice that despite its softness took nothing away from its lethal intent. 'I am not going to fall in love with you. I made that clear from the beginning. I've seen what loving someone does to you. It makes you weak, selfish and stupid. I'm not going to do that. Ever. And if you think it might happen by accident, if you think you can change me or make me love you, you are wrong. Wrong.' He paused, his gaze steady on her, making sure she understood.

Rhiannon felt the colour drain from her face. She was too horrified, too stricken to speak or even to blush. The terrible finality of his tone seemed to reverberate through her bones, through her soul, making a mockery of every fragile hope she'd just begun to cherish.

'I'm sorry,' Lukas said, more gently now. 'I thought you understood that. I thought I'd made it clear.'

Rhiannon gave a slight, self-protective shake of her head. When she spoke, it was through stiff, numb lips. 'You did.' She struggled up from the stone, shrugged away Lukas's hand and began the long, stony walk back to the village.

They returned to the hotel in silence, the easy and enjoyable banter of only a few hours ago now replaced with a taut tension. They packed up their few things stiffly, jerkily, before heading back to the boat.

Once on board, Rhiannon curled in a seat as far away from Lukas as she could. She didn't want to watch him, to see the long, rippling muscles of his shoulders and back while he hauled on the sails. Didn't want to replay the words that he'd spoken so flatly, so mercilessly, on the hill.

Yet they kept replaying anyway, a remorseless echo in her brain, reminding her that once again, as always, she'd begged for love and been refused.

Love made you strong.

She'd felt strong last night. In Lukas's arms she'd revelled in the power of their joined bodies, joined hearts. Except it had to have been false. Because there was no power, no strength, no joy in her current agony, in Lukas's flat rejection, in knowing once again she was where she'd been her whole life: living as someone's burden.

Lukas watched Rhiannon out of the corner of his eye, his hand resting on the jib. She was curled up like a whipped puppy, her face closed in on itself, her eyes gazing unseeingly at the stretch of sea before them.

Guilt assailed him, stabbed him with tiny needles. He didn't need this. Hadn't wanted it.

Yet he deserved it.

He'd acted selfishly, wanting Rhiannon's body without her heart. Wanting her to enter a loveless marriage when she'd admitted she wanted love more than anything else.

He'd pushed aside her objections, her desires, in preference of his own. He wanted her. He recognised that—admitted that it hadn't been responsibility for anyone that had driven him to marry her. It had been need. Desire.

He just didn't want to love her, and he certainly didn't want her to love him.

She would learn, Lukas told himself. She would realise that desire and affection were better than love. She would come round.

And if she didn't...? Lukas smiled savagely, his face averted from his bride.

There were no other options. Not for either of them. He wouldn't let there be.

When the boat came in sight of the Petrakides island, Adeia was already coming from the villa towards the dock, her apron blowing in the breeze.

Anxiety clutched at Rhiannon's heart, tightened around it like a vice. 'Is something wrong?'

'I don't know.' Lukas's face was filled with foreboding, and Rhiannon realised that the problem—if there was one—might just as easily concern Theo as Annabel.

'Master Lukas,' Adeia called breathlessly as Lukas tied up the boat. 'I've been looking for your boat all morning—"

'What's happened, Adeia?' Rhiannon cut in. 'Is it Annabel? Theo?'

'Neither. Master Lukas, your sister arrived last night. She is insistent that she take the baby with her.'

Lukas swore under his breath before jumping nimbly from the boat. He turned to help Rhiannon down, then excused himself.

'I must go and see Antonia.'

'I'm coming too.'

He shook his head in swift denial. 'This does not concern you, Rhiannon—'

'It absolutely concerns me,' she retorted. 'That's why we married, remember? I'm as involved as you are, Lukas, so *don't* shut me out now.'

Lukas gave a terse nod. 'So be it.'

Antonia was in the lounge when they entered the villa. She was a tall, thin woman, expertly made up, but with a sharpened hardness to her that came from years of dissolute and disappointed living.

'Hello, Antonia.' Lukas spoke with a calm cordiality that Rhiannon doubted anyone in the room was close to feeling.

Antonia put her hands on her bony hips. She wore an expensive suit in a glaring shade of pink—something chic and completely unsuitable for either island living or life with a baby.

'Christos told me everything, Lukas. I want her.' Her eyes flashed, and Rhiannon felt her own blaze at the woman's tone, wheedling and greedy, as if she were demanding a sweet.

'I'm afraid,' Lukas said mildly, 'that it's not going to be that simple.'

'Why not? I'm her grandmother, her closest living relative

besides Christos, and he supports me taking her. You'll find he'll stand with me in court.'

'Antonia, do you really want to drag us all—and the Petrakides name—into court?'

'I don't give a damn about the Petrakides name,' Antonia spat. 'That's just you and Father. Both of you care more about the idea of our wretched family than the people in it—no wonder Mama left when she could, grabbed happiness when she found it.'

Unmoved, a muscle ticking in his jaw, Lukas raised one eyebrow. 'As you have? With drugs, drink, and far too many lovers?'

Colour blazed in Antonia's cheeks and she shot Rhiannon an angry, furtive glance before shrugging. 'I've put such ways behind me now, Lukas. You'll find I have quite a collection of witnesses to testify to that fact. And any judge will understand how I was driven to what I did because my own home life was so appalling!'

'Spare me the theatrics, please, Antonia. No one cares about your poor little rich girl story.'

Antonia thrust her chin out. 'Don't you think, Lukas, that a judge will be more sympathetic to a close relative who is willing to love this child than to someone who takes it because he doesn't want scandal to stain his precious name?'

The jibe hit home, for Lukas's face went white and he spoke stiffly. 'We'll just to have see... Unless you are willing to see sense and drop this farce right now. I know you don't really care about Christos's child. You haven't even met her.'

'I do care!' Antonia shrieked. She looked near tears, and Rhiannon felt a stab of sympathy for the woman, distraught as she clearly was. 'I *will* care. You might not need anyone to love, but I do. I *do!*'

This last ended on a wail of desperation. Rhiannon's heart was tugged in spite of her intentions to remain unmoved. Antonia was so obviously unhappy—needy enough to convince herself that a baby would provide her with purpose and pleasure.

Antonia took a deep breath, composed herself. 'A judge will rule—'

'Against a stable married couple with the child's best interests at heart? I don't think so.'

Antonia's mouth opened, closed. 'Married?' she repeated. 'But who…?' Things clicked into place and she turned a furious, disbelieving stare on Rhiannon. 'You married this English nobody? For the sake of a child you don't even care about? You do take your duty seriously, Lukas, don't you?'

'Yes,' he replied in a tight, controlled voice. 'I do.'

She flung her head back, her face bright with hectic colour. 'We'll see what the judge says.'

'I hope it doesn't come to that, for all our sakes, Antonia.'

'You mean for *your* sake,' she threw back, and Lukas gave a tiny shrug.

'You're welcome to stay, of course, but perhaps it might be prudent for you to return to London.'

'You want me gone already?' Antonia jeered. 'I don't want to stay anyway. But I'll return to Athens, Lukas. As you know this case will be tried in a Greek court. And then we'll see…won't we?' She turned her vitriolic gaze on Rhiannon. 'I don't know if you married him for the kid or the money, but I promise you, you will be unhappy.'

Then, with an angry click of heels, she was gone.

Rhiannon was silent, recovering from the violence of the encounter, the words still pouring through her like acid.

You will be unhappy.

It had almost sounded like a curse.

In the distance, she heard the sound of a helicopter lifting off, and sagged slightly in relief. She was gone.

'I'm sorry about that.' Lukas finally spoke into the silence. 'I told you what she was like, but I had no idea she'd be so vicious.'

'Desperate,' Rhiannon corrected quietly. 'She's unhappy, Lukas.'

He shook his head. 'By her own hand. She makes more trouble for herself than anyone else possibly could.'

Rhiannon lifted her head, met his cold, steely gaze. 'Can't you find it in your heart to feel sorry for her?'

'Sorry?' Lukas raised his eyebrows in incredulity. 'Rhiannon, this is the woman who wants to take Annabel away from you—from us! And she'll lie, cheat and steal to do it. Why should you feel sorry for her?'

Rhiannon shrugged. 'I don't applaud her methods, but she's obviously desperate for love. She thinks a baby will somehow provide meaning in her life. At one time I wasn't that different, you know.'

'You were willing to give Annabel up,' Lukas objected. 'You can hardly compare yourself to Antonia!'

'I was willing to marry a stranger,' Rhiannon snapped, 'to stay with her! Don't think you know me so well, Lukas.'

He gazed at her for a moment. 'Is that what I am? A stranger?'

'Sometimes you feel like one,' Rhiannon admitted, trying to keep her voice steady and cool. 'Even if I don't want it to be that way.'

'I told you what this marriage would be like,' he said, an angry, impatient edge turning his voice sharp. 'I warned you that I wouldn't love you. I don't have that to give, Rhiannon. Full stop.'

'I know, Lukas.' She felt quite suddenly unbearably weary, tired of this argument that went in endless circles because they wanted different things and couldn't understand how the other could want what they didn't.

Or, in Lukas's case, want anything at all.

He wanted nothing…except maybe her body.

'I need to check on Annabel,' she said, her voice toneless and flat.

Reluctantly Lukas let her go.

'I'll need to go to Athens tomorrow morning,' he said. 'I've left my business too long, and if Antonia is going to make trouble I need to be on hand.'

Rhiannon shrugged her acceptance.

'I want you to come with me.'

She turned in surprise. She'd expected to remain on the island, not to interfere with Lukas's business, with his life. 'You do?'

'We're *married,* Rhiannon.' Lukas spoke patiently. 'I want you with me. I want you in my bed, by my side.'

In his bed. He made it so wonderfully clear. 'Fine. Annabel comes too.'

'Of course.'

She turned away, walked up the stairs, and felt Lukas's restless gaze burning into her back.

Annabel was delighted to see her. With the baby chortling on her hip, Rhiannon went to check on Theo.

He was propped up in bed, his cheeks still sunken, his hair lank and dry, but his eyes glinted brightly and he smiled when he saw her.

'How was the honeymoon? Short, I fear?'

'Long enough,' Rhiannon replied, and Theo frowned.

'What is wrong?'

'Nothing.' She smiled, setting Annabel on the floor so she could check his vitals. 'Has the doctor been?'

'Yes. I'm stable for the moment. Don't fuss over me. What is wrong? What has happened?'

Rhiannon smiled down at him. Somehow, in some strange way, she'd become fond of Theo—and, even more oddly, he'd become fond of her. She didn't know why—didn't know if it was just because she was the female Lukas had been willing to marry, or if the affection was based on something deeper.

She knew Theo wanted them to be happy, just as she did. But she couldn't make Lukas love her.

She'd learned that lesson a long time ago, when she'd been the sweetest, most polite, most obedient little girl in the world, and it hadn't made her parents soften at all. They hadn't wanted her; they'd done their duty and, like a canker, it had festered slowly into resentment until everything she'd done had become an irritation, an annoyance. A burden.

Did you ever love me?

I tried.

She'd begun to believe things could change, that she could change Lukas. She'd begun to believe in love again. In someone loving her.

But it wasn't going to happen, Rhiannon thought sadly. And,

like her parents, Lukas would start to resent her when the desire faded, when he'd had enough of her body. There'd be nothing left but the burden.

'Well?' Theo demanded, and she managed a smile.

'Theo, you know our marriage wasn't a love match. We're doing as well as we can.'

'But you care for each other?' Theo insisted, and Rhiannon wondered how to answer that.

Care for each other? She loved Lukas—loved his strength, the way he made her feel safe, the feel of his arms around her. Loved the little boy he'd been, the boy she hoped he still was underneath, determined to guard his heart so damn carefully.

'Rhiannon…' Theo reached for her hand. 'You must give him time. He's spent thirty-one years of his life trying not to love anyone.' Theo smiled sadly. 'I taught him that. After Paulina— my wife—left I hardened my heart. I hardened Lukas's too.'

Rhiannon's heart ached at the regret in Theo's voice. 'What about your daughters?' she asked, thinking of Antonia, her desperation and her bitterness.

Theo shrugged. 'They were older, and more like their mother. They understood why she left but I refused to. I made sure Lukas refused to, as well.'

'Why did she leave, do you think?' Rhiannon asked quietly, and Theo's eyes hardened briefly before he shrugged.

'I thought we had the same dream…to build the Petrakides business, to establish a name for ourselves and our children. That wasn't enough for her. She found what she wanted with a racing car driver—a fool who gave her false promises. But she believed them, and they made her happy…for a little while.'

The long speech had exhausted him, and he lay back against the pillows, his face haggard and grey.

'You should rest now,' Rhiannon said. She tucked the covers around his gaunt frame before picking up Annabel and slipping quietly from the room.

Sighing, she returned to her bedroom to settle Annabel for her afternoon nap.

She laid the baby on her back on the bed, tickling her tummy and smiling as Annabel kicked her feet and waved her starfish hands enthusiastically.

'You seem to have done all right without me,' she said, and she blew a raspberry on Annabel's tummy. 'Miss me much, sweetheart?'

Annabel gurgled in response, and Rhiannon heard a quiet voice from the door.

'She obviously adores you.'

She froze, then turned to see Lukas leaning against the door-frame, a look of tender wistfulness on his face. The breath caught and dried in Rhiannon's throat at that look...the look of a man who desperately wanted something.

Wanted love.

She gave herself a mental shake—because, no matter how much her heart wanted to believe that was true, Lukas had given her his opinion on the subject, and she wasn't quite naive enough to believe she could change him.

Was she?

'Do you want to hold her?' She scooped Annabel up. 'She's just been changed, so this is a good time.'

'All right.' Gingerly Lukas took hold of her, his arms going around her awkwardly but with increasing confidence. Annabel laughed and reached up to pat both of his cheeks.

This is our family, Rhiannon thought with a strange sweet pang. *Our family.* Her throat suddenly felt tight, and her eyes stung. Because that seemed like a lot just then.

She'd never had a proper family before—and neither, it seemed, had Lukas.

'She has the Petrakides look,' Lukas said as he smoothed Annabel's dusky curls back from her forehead. 'It's in the eyes.'

Annabel tugged hard on Lukas's ear and he captured her little hand in his. 'Easy, *thisavre mou,*' he said with a little laugh.

At his gentle rebuke, Annabel screwed up her face and burst into noisy tears.

Lukas looked stricken.

Rhiannon smothered a laugh. 'She's just tired. I was about to put her down for a nap.'

'It will take some time for her to get used to me,' Lukas admitted ruefully as he handed her back to Rhiannon. 'For us all to get used to each other.'

Rhiannon nodded, accepting the peace offering. 'Yes,' she agreed, 'it's all very strange.'

Lukas glanced around the room. 'I'll have your things moved into my bedroom this afternoon. Annabel can be in the room adjoining.'

'I thought we were going to Athens tomorrow,' Rhiannon protested. 'It's hardly neces—'

'It is,' Lukas said firmly. 'Because I want it to be so.'

'I thought,' she retorted acerbically, 'you didn't want anything.'

'I want you, and I'll have you,' Lukas replied. 'Tonight.'

Rhiannon glared. 'Do you have to be so base?'

'What is base about us loving each other as husband and wife?'

'Because it's not about love, Lukas. Remember?'

Annabel cried again, and Rhiannon turned away. 'I need to put her down for a nap.'

Lukas nodded tersely before turning on his heel. Rhiannon heard rather than saw the door click shut.

She put the baby to bed, doing her best to suppress the fury that boiled through her.

He'd have her, would he? Did he have to make it so appallingly clear that it was simply sex for him?

Desire. Lust.

Later that night, after Annabel was settled in her new room and Theo had been seen to, Rhiannon knew there was no putting it off.

She'd busied herself away from Lukas for most of the day, unable to see him without hurting, without wanting. More. Yet she knew this was the bargain he'd offered—a bargain she'd accepted. One she'd thought she could live with.

It was her own fault—her own problem—if now she found she couldn't.

When she finally approached the bedroom to where he'd had all her things moved—*his* bedroom—she found it empty.

An irritating disappointment settled over her as she surveyed the wide, empty bed—the cream-coloured duvet smooth and untouched, the pillows plumped.

The room was furnished in dark wood and light colours. A masculine room. When Rhiannon took a breath, she inhaled Lukas's scent, that achingly familiar mixture of soap and pine, pure male.

She paused on the threshold, uncertain what to do. Go to bed by herself? Wait for Lukas?

Everything was so new, so strange.

After a moment's indecision she went back downstairs, following her instinct, her heart, to the lounge.

The door was closed, just as before, and she couldn't hear a sound, but somehow she knew.

She pushed it open with her fingertips, saw him at the piano. His head was bowed over the instrument, his fingers poised on the keys without touching them.

He looked, Rhiannon thought, anguished.

'Lukas…?'

He looked up when he saw her, his expression turning guarded, blank.

'I thought you'd be asleep.'

'I was waiting for you,' Rhiannon confessed, and he raised an eyebrow.

'Why? You made it clear earlier that you did not want me with you tonight.'

'I…' She stopped, licked her lips. 'I do want you with me,' she admitted. 'I just don't like it to sound so…base.'

'But to you,' Lukas replied, his tone almost musing, his fingers rippling discordantly over the keys, 'it *is* base. Because I don't love you. I'll never satisfy you, will I, Rhiannon? I'll never please you because I can't give you what you most want.'

The raw truth of it made her blink, stare. She'd expected him to admit it, she supposed. She just hadn't expected him to sound as if it made him sad.

As if it hurt.

'We can try to be happy,' she said after a moment, but she heard the hollow ring of her words. 'For Annabel's sake.'

'And for our own?'

'Yes…' she said.

He nodded slowly. 'I've done the right thing all my life. The responsible thing, the thing everyone told me was my duty. I've lived by it. And I convinced myself I'd done that with you. But maybe I just wanted you. Maybe I made a mistake.'

'If you did, it's already done,' Rhiannon replied. 'Unless you want a divorce?' Why did that thought make her nearly nauseous? She didn't want to leave Lukas.

She just didn't know if she could stay with him.

'No,' Lukas said quietly, 'I don't want a divorce. I'll never want a divorce.'

Even if they were both miserable, Rhiannon thought. Lukas would never shirk his responsibility in such a way. He would never bring a single blemish to the family name.

Yet the strangely lost look on his face reminded her of the boy he'd been—the boy whose mother had walked out on him when he was only five, the boy who'd been told not to love anyone.

This was the man she loved.

She moved closer to him, knelt by his side. Lukas looked down at her, smiling slightly sadly at her in a way that made Rhiannon ache. Want.

She reached up to place her hands on either side of his face, to draw him to her for a kiss. A kiss that was meant to be tender, gentle. Healing.

Lukas broke the kiss first, leaning his forehead against hers. He sighed softly.

'Let's go to bed,' Rhiannon whispered, and she led him by the hand, upstairs, to the room they now shared.

He stood by the window, still and silent, watching her with that same sweet sorrow.

'You don't have to—' he began.

Rhiannon shook her head. 'I want to.' She slipped out of her clothes before turning to him, unbuttoning his shirt, sliding off his trousers.

Lukas pulled her to him. 'I want you,' he groaned against her mouth. 'I need you.'

As he laid her gently on the bed, his hands stroking and caressing her with an urgency Rhiannon felt kindle in her own soul, she knew that would have to be enough.

It was all Lukas had to give.

The next morning Lukas was gone from the bedroom when Rhiannon awoke, tangled in the sheets and feeling bereft by his absence.

He soon appeared with a tray of coffee and rolls, which he set on the table by the bed. 'Annabel's still sleeping, but we need to leave for Athens within the hour.'

'So soon?' Rhiannon said in concern, for the deep frown between Lukas's dark brow told its own story.

'Yes. I've just had word that Christos joined his mother in Athens yesterday. With the two of them determined to cause trouble together, we need to sort this out as soon as possible. I'm quite sure Antonia will drop this ridiculous custody case when she sees its futility, but I'd prefer the press not to get wind of it. Then we can start adoption proceedings for Annabel.'

Rhiannon nodded. There were so many obstacles to overcome, yet at least they would do it together. Lukas had said 'we'.

The flight to Athens was brief, and Rhiannon spent most of her time settling Annabel.

A limousine met them at the airport, whisking them to Lukas's villa in Drosia, a suburb to the north of Athens, in the pine forests at the foot of the Penteli mountains.

'I'm sorry to leave you here,' Lukas said when Rhiannon and the baby had been unloaded from the car. 'but I must go directly to the office. The staff will make you comfortable in the meantime.'

'All right,' Rhiannon said, accepting the reality, yet feeling a bit hesitant about the sudden rapid changes.

Lukas pressed a hard kiss on her mouth. 'Tonight.'

Rhiannon could only nod. 'I hope it all goes well.'

She watched the car disappear down the long, twisting drive, swallowed up by the dense pine forests flanking the narrow lane.

She turned towards the house, an impressive villa that looked as if it had been built into the mountainside, or had sprung from the very stone.

She opened the front door, stepped into the tiled foyer.

'Hello...?' Her voice echoed into the empty space.

Then she heard the tapping of feet, and a man appeared in the doorway. He was dark, slim, handsome in a laconic way, and he smiled at her in a manner Rhiannon didn't like.

'You must be the English nobody,' he said pleasantly. 'I doubt you were expecting me—nor was my dear uncle, for that matter. I'm Christos.'

CHAPTER TEN

RHIANNON'S arms tightened around Annabel as a matter of instinct. This was Annabel's father. The man she'd come to Greece to find.

Yet now she wanted him gone.

'Lukas has just left,' she said when she finally found her voice. 'If you wanted to speak to him.'

'I did,' Christos agreed, 'but I suppose I can speak to you instead.'

'All right,' Rhiannon agreed evenly. 'If this is about your mother and her custody case—'

'Oh, that.' Christos laughed—an unkind trill. 'She's dropped that. She's halfway back to London by now, I should think.'

'But...' Rhiannon's head spun as hope and suspicion clashed and tangled. 'Are you serious? I spoke to her only yesterday—'

'My mother is—as I am—capricious.' Christos smiled. 'I asked for a drink from that slouch of a housekeeper, but she hasn't brought it yet. Would you care for anything?'

'No,' Rhiannon said stiffly. 'I'm fine.'

'Are you?' Christos laughed again and led the way into the lounge.

Rhiannon followed him on wooden legs. She had a growing sense of dread, an icy pooling in her middle, and she wasn't even sure why.

The lounge was an airy, spacious room, and Christos sat on one sofa, indicating that Rhiannon should take the other. She did, and though Annabel squirmed to get down, Rhiannon kept her firmly on her lap.

'So why did you marry Lukas?' Christos asked in a musing way. 'Or should I ask why did he marry you?'

'To provide a stable home for Annabel,' Rhiannon replied. 'A child should have two parents.'

'More than I had,' Christos agreed. 'More than Lukas had, for that matter.'

'What do you know about that?'

He shrugged. 'My grandmother left when he was five. But you've been told that, I suppose? Apparently Lukas didn't speak for nearly a month after she was gone.' He laughed. 'He was that shaken up! Then, when he finally did speak, he sounded like a parrot of my sainted grandfather.' His mouth twisted in a cruel smile. 'My mother has never had time for him, and neither do I.'

Rhiannon pressed her lips together. 'Do you know your grandfather is very ill?' she asked, and Christos shrugged.

'My mother mentioned it, but nobody really cares. Why should we? He's hardly done right by us.'

'I suppose that's why no one has visited,' Rhiannon said stiffly, and he laughed.

'I'll see that old bastard at his funeral, with his money in my fist.'

She shook her head, unable to quite believe his callousness, or his clear delight in shocking her. 'Why are you here, Christos?'

'Well…' He leaned forward. 'I wanted to tell Uncle Lukas the news. See the look on his face. The horror! He's always done his damn duty, and hated us for it, and now he's done it again and he didn't even have to.' He chuckled. 'Won't that just kill him?'

The cold, the dread, were intensifying. Rhiannon's hands tightened around Annabel, and she squawked in protest.

'What are you talking about?'

'I wonder why Lukas married you,' Christos continued, ignoring her question. 'He clearly didn't have to. It was a drastic measure, even for him. But I can't really believe he wanted to, either.' The once-over he gave her was both blatant and dismissive, and had Rhiannon gritting her teeth.

'Maybe you should just leave.'

'Oh, I will. This place is out in the sticks. I much prefer the family flat in Athens. But I'll tell you my news—before I stop by and tell Lukas too.' He jerked a contemptuous thumb towards Annabel. 'She's not mine.'

'What?' Rhiannon stared blankly. It was the last thing she'd been expecting.

'She's not mine,' Christos repeated. 'I finally got around to taking the paternity test, and the results came back today. There's ninety-nine per cent chance we're not related.' His smile widened. 'So I don't know who that brat belongs to, but it's not me...or anyone in the Petrakides family.'

'But you spent the weekend with Leanne,' Rhiannon said numbly.

'I did. But she obviously found someone else as well. We didn't spend every moment together, you know. By the time we'd got on the plane I was already a bit bored.'

Rhiannon shook her head, refusing to believe. To accept. 'She spoke so warmly of you...'

'Did she? We had a good time, I suppose. It seems she had a good time with someone else too.'

Was it possible? Rhiannon wondered. It had to be. Yet why would Leanne...?

She'd been desperate to believe, Rhiannon supposed. Leanne had thought Christos was a good man, a rich man. One who could provide for her daughter. Perhaps she'd wanted Rhiannon to find him. When you were unhappy and desperate, you could convince yourself of almost anything.

As she nearly had...like Lukas being able to love. *Her.* So who on earth was Annabel's father? Rhiannon wondered. Another man Leanne had met in Naxos—or someone before or after?

She would never know.

Christos rose elegantly from the sofa. 'Sorry to be the bearer of bad news,' he said, without even a breath of regret. 'I wonder what will happen now? A quickie divorce? Or will Lukas stand by you, no matter how much it hurts? That should be interesting to see.'

Rhiannon couldn't form a reply. Her mind was too numb, too frozen. Annabel squirmed again, and with unsteady hands she set her on the floor.

The front door clicked shut.

She was alone in a strange house, in a strange city, with a stranger's child.

She looked down at Annabel. She loved her, no matter who her father was—or wasn't.

She doubted Lukas would feel the same.

How many times had he told her he would do his duty to a child *of his blood?*

Not some changeling he had no connection to!

A bubble of hysterical laughter rose to her lips. She pressed a fist to her mouth, willing it down. Willing herself to be calm.

Annabel was not a Petrakides. Yet they were still married. Lukas would never agree to a divorce; he'd said as much. She was tied to him—tied to him for no reason but his own inflated sense of responsibility. For her.

A burden.

There was no reason for them to be married now.

No reason at all.

Had there ever been?

Rhiannon stilled even as her mind whirled. Christos had expressed surprise that Lukas had been willing to marry her, to go so far to protect Annabel's future.

Even Rhiannon hadn't seen the necessity for such drastic measures, and yet she'd accepted them. She'd agreed.

Why?

Because I loved him, she acknowledged, *even then.*

Because she'd believed he could change. That she could change him.

Why had Lukas agreed? Was it just responsibility…or something more? Could she hope? Could she challenge him, confront him?

How could she not? Her heart began a steady thud.

Love made you strong.

She leaned her head against the back of the sofa, closing her eyes. It was such a risk…

It was worth it. It had to be.

A tentative knock sounded at the door.

'Master Christos…?' The housekeeper, a slight woman, with grey hair scraped back in a bun, holding a drink on a tray, stood in the doorway.

'He's left,' Rhiannon explained, then smiled wearily. 'But I'll take that drink.'

The villa was cloaked in darkness when Rhiannon finally heard Lukas's car come up the drive. It had been a long, painful afternoon; she'd endured hours of wondering, questioning, fearing, hoping.

After a fretful afternoon Annabel had fallen asleep in her car seat, as there was no travel cot in the villa.

It was just as well, Rhiannon thought, considering what she might have to do. What she was willing to do.

Her life and her heart were on the line.

The front door opened, and she heard his soft, steady tread.

'Rhiannon…?' He came into the lounge, saw her standing in the middle of the room, and his face turned to stone.

'What are those?'

'My bags,' Rhiannon said flatly. She nudged a suitcase at her foot. 'I trust Christos found you?'

'Yes, he did.' Lukas raked a hand through his hair.

'So you know?'

'If you mean about Annabel—'

'You said she looked like a Petrakides!' Rhiannon couldn't keep the note of accusation, of hurt, out of her voice.

'I suppose,' Lukas said heavily, 'I wanted it to be true.' He looked at the suitcases by Rhiannon's feet. 'But why—?'

'If Annabel isn't Christos's baby, Lukas, then she's not related to you. She's not…' Rhiannon took a breath, dragging it desperately into her lungs. 'Your responsibility.'

Lukas was silent for a moment, studying her. 'She is now,' he finally said. 'As you are.'

'That's where you're wrong. I've never wanted to be your responsibility. You tried to make me into some wretched duty, but I won't accept it, Lukas. I have my own life, and you're not responsible for it.'

'You're my wife,' Lukas said flatly, as if that ended the discussion.

'We can get divorced.' Rhiannon forced herself to ignore the look of furious incredulity that slashed across his features. 'Or have the marriage annulled.'

'Annulled? On what grounds?'

She shrugged. 'A fancy solicitor could find some reason, I'm sure.'

He shook his head slowly. 'No.'

'No? Just like that? You can't order me—'

'There will be no divorce.' His voice was so flat, his expression so cold, that Rhiannon felt her nerve begin to desert her.

What on earth was she doing?

'Then I'll leave.'

He paused, raised one eyebrow. 'In the middle of the night? With Annabel?'

'She's asleep in her car seat. I can call a taxi.'

'You don't speak Greek.'

Rhiannon's smile was brittle. 'I've found an English-speaking service already.' She held up the mobile he'd given her. 'It's on speed dial.'

Lukas shook his head slowly. 'You won't leave.'

'Try me.' Her heart was pounding, her face flushed, her mouth dry. She didn't *want* to leave, but she would if it came to it. If Lukas forced her.

'Let me make myself clear,' Lukas said, and his voice was ominously calm. 'You are not *allowed* to leave.'

'I don't care how powerful you are, Lukas, you can't keep me here. And I'll tell you right now—the only way I'd stay is if you loved me.'

He froze, stared at her in incredulity. 'Love? That's what this is about? I have already told you, Rhiannon—'

'I know what you said. I know what we agreed. But things have changed, Lukas. *I've* changed. And this is the way it is now.'

'You ask too much!'

'Do I?' Her smile was sad. 'There's no reason for us to be married, Lukas, except for love. Don't you see that? We can't use Annabel as a reason or as an excuse.'

'Excuse?' he repeated furiously, and she lifted her chin.

'I'm not going to stay married to you simply because you can't have a blemish on your family name. My life—my love—is worth more than that.'

Lukas's face was white, his eyes blazing silver. 'You will not divorce me, Rhiannon.'

The quiet warning in his voice made her only more determined. 'Tell me why not, then, Lukas.'

'Because we're married, and I honour my vows,' he said through gritted teeth. 'Now, I've had quite enough of this discussion…' He turned to leave the room.

'I haven't.' Rhiannon grabbed his arm, pulled him towards her. He froze, swivelled slowly.

'What do you want from me?' His voice was stony, cold, yet she heard—felt—the frayed edges, and knew he was losing control of that remote, icy demeanour. She wanted it stripped away. She wanted him bare, as bare as she was, with her emotions, her heart splayed open.

'Your love. I love you, Lukas.'

He looked at her, nonplussed and silent. Rhiannon felt the humiliation, the pain, the rejection, and forced herself not to give in. She took a breath.

'I won't stay in a marriage without love.'

'You should have thought of that before you took your vows,' Lukas replied coldly. 'Now I'm going to bed.'

Rhiannon watched him stalk out of the room, her heart thudding dully against her ribs, her pulse rushing in her ears. She was going about this all wrong. She'd wanted to draw a confession from him, a declaration, but it wasn't happening.

She was just making him angry.

With leaden steps she walked upstairs, found Lukas in the bedroom, tugging off his tie. She watched him sadly, feeling so far away from him, so distant from his emotions, his thoughts, his heart.

And she wanted to be close. She wanted to be so close.

Lukas glanced up and saw her. 'Coming to bed?' he queried sardonically, and Rhiannon shrugged.

'Is that where you want me?'

His eyes glinted. 'It's a start.'

Rhiannon swallowed. 'Fine.' She strode to the foot of the bed and began to undress. It was a deliberate, brutal striptease, designed not to seduce but to shame. Shame them both.

She unbuttoned her blouse, slipped it off her shoulders, shrugged off her jeans.

Lukas watched, a muscle ticking in his jaw, his face impassive.

She hesitated for a second before slipping off her underwear. She stood there naked while Lukas watched, arms crossed.

'Is this what you want?' she demanded. 'My body? Sex? Nothing else? Is that enough for you?' She lay on the bed, spread her thighs. 'Then take it, Lukas. And maybe you'll see how empty it is without love.'

Distaste flickered in his eyes. 'You're acting like a whore.'

'No,' she retorted, 'you're treating me like one.'

She lay there naked, exposed, open. Knowing this was how it must be. She couldn't demand that Lukas share his weakness, his truth, if she didn't share hers.

'It was good between us,' he told her, and with calculated tenderness he moved his hand up her calf, towards her thigh. 'I could make you want me even now.'

'Yes, you could.' Her voice trembled as his hand slid further, teased her. She saw the desire dilating his pupils, making his breath come quicker, as hers was.

He dropped his hand and turned away. His tie was loosened, his shirt half unbuttoned as he raked a hand through his hair. 'Why can't that be enough for you?'

'Because I want you to love me.' She sat up, still naked, unashamed. 'And I think you do. You may have been pretending otherwise—'

Her voice trembled, and Lukas shook his head in disbelief. 'If anyone is pretending, Rhiannon, it's you.'

She hoped that wasn't true. She desperately wanted it not to be true.

Now she needed to be bold. She needed to beg.

'Lukas, I love you.'

He shook his head—a violent movement of instinctive denial. 'No—'

'And you love me.'

The silence was terrifying. He stared at her. His face was cold, as if carved from ice, from stone, his eyes hard. Dead. 'No.' He spoke so flatly, so finally, that Rhiannon almost considered giving up.

Almost.

'Christos wondered why you married me,' she said, her voice a thread. A thread of steel. 'Why you felt you needed to—'

'For Annabel,' Lukas cut across her. 'Let's not rehash this, Rhiannon. It will only become painful…for you.'

'Too late.' She tried to smile, felt the tears. 'The thing is, Lukas, Christos got me thinking. Thinking things I'd already begun to wonder about. To hope for. You didn't need to marry me to secure Annabel's future. You said yourself that Antonia was fickle, that she might drop the custody case simply because she was bored. A judge would not even have considered her suit seriously, despite any witnesses she brought forward. Marriage was an extreme reaction—even for you.'

'Was it?' He stood still, his arms hanging by his sides, his hands loose, yet Rhiannon could feel the tension in him, knew he wanted to clench his fists.

'Yes. And I went along with it. I let you convince me because I wanted to marry you. I loved you even then—even though I was afraid you'd end up hurting me because you wouldn't love me back.'

'As I am now?' He hissed. 'Rhiannon, if you're trying to convince yourself—'

'Maybe I am.' Her voice wavered, broke. 'Look at me, Lukas. Look at me here, naked, on my knees, doing the one thing I swore I would never do again. Begging for love.' She shook her head, tears rolling slowly down her cheeks. 'You know why I'm doing it? Why I'm letting myself? Because love is *strong,* Lukas. Love makes you strong. Even here, begging as I am, I feel strong. I *am* strong. Because I love you. And I know that's a good thing, a beautiful thing, that will never weaken or destroy me.'

He began to shake his head. Stopped. There was an anguished, arrested look in his eyes, as if he wanted to stop listening, to deny what she said, what he felt.

There would be no stopping now.

'Christos told me about your mother. How she left and you didn't speak for a month.'

'Don't—' It came out as a harsh cry, and yet still she continued.

'She hurt you—more than anyone else could—and you've never wanted it to happen again. Don't let her win, Lukas. Don't let her keep you from loving.'

He strode towards her, grabbed her arms and hauled her to her feet. 'You know nothing! *Nothing!*' he said savagely and then kissed her, hard. It was a demand, a punishment. 'This is all we'll have. All we'll ever have. It's all I have to give, Rhiannon, so stop doing this!' His voice broke, surprising them both, and he pushed her away. '*Stop.*' It came out as a plea, his shoulders hunched, his face averted.

'I'll stop,' Rhiannon said quietly. She didn't bother to wipe the tears that streaked silently down her cheeks, didn't hide the ache of longing and sorrow in her voice. 'I'll stop when you look at me and tell me you don't love me. Look me in the face—in my eyes—and say those words.'

'*Fine!*' He turned towards her, his face filled with fury, with despair. He opened his mouth and Rhiannon's heart began to break. 'I don't—' He stopped, snapped his mouth closed, and strode to the window. His back was to her, and she could see tension, anguish, in every taut line of his body.

She held her breath, her cheeks still damp, and waited. The silence stretched between them, aching and expectant.

'When my mother was going to leave,' Lukas began, in a strange, distant voice, 'I heard her talking to my father.'

He stopped, his face still averted, his body still thrumming with tension. Rhiannon took a shallow breath and kept on waiting.

'She told him that she loved Milo. Her lover. She said she hadn't known what love was till she met him. That he made her feel happy and alive.' He shook his head slowly. 'I didn't understand what he was talking about, of course. I was only five. But I thought that *I* loved her as much as this Milo did.' He paused, raking a hand through his hair before dropping it. 'My father pleaded with her to stay. He was…pitiful. Even as a five-year-old I realised that, and I was embarrassed for him. Of course I didn't realise my mother was leaving me at that point. I never thought she would leave *me*.'

His voice choked slightly, and he kept his face turned away from her. After a long, ragged moment, he continued.

'I saw her go down the stairs. Milo was waiting outside. My father said she would lose us—the children—and after only a second she said, "I don't care."' He laughed—a short, sharp sound. 'I couldn't believe it. I ran up to her, told her to take me with her. I couldn't believe she'd be willing to leave me…that she'd want to. Of course now I realise Milo wouldn't have wanted the encumbrance of four children. My mother was very beautiful, but she was still ten years older than he was, and she needed to do everything she could to keep him.'

'What happened then?' Rhiannon asked in a whisper, when it seemed as if Lukas wouldn't continue.

'I was every bit as pitiful as my father.' His voice was flat, toneless. 'I begged, I pleaded, I sobbed. I clung to her legs, her shoes. She kicked me off. She said, "Take him."'

Rhiannon closed her eyes briefly, pain slashing through her as she thought of what Lukas had gone through. What he was going through now, remembering.

'I don't remember how they got me off her. I don't even remember her leaving. But I never saw her again.'

'Lukas…'

He shook his head, flinging up one hand to keep her from speaking. 'My three sisters were in school or out on their own at that point. I'd been a late and unexpected addition. It was just my father and me, and he shaped me in the pattern of his own deep bitterness. I don't blame him, because I was already bitter…even as a child. I vowed to never let that happen to me again.'

He turned to face her, and Rhiannon's heart twisted, expanded at the bleak honesty on his face.

'So, you see, Rhiannon, I've lied to you. I lied in telling you that I wouldn't love anyone because I'd seen how it weakened and cheapened others. It isn't *others* that have kept me from giving my heart, it's been myself. *I* was weakened…cheapened. I wanted to protect myself from that happening again.' He smiled—a painful twisting of his lips. 'The trouble is, I haven't been able to keep myself from falling in love. I've fought it every step of the way— lied to myself about why I wanted to be with you, even why I needed to marry you. I insisted to myself it was a matter of responsibility— yes, wretched duty—but it wasn't. It was a matter of love.'

'Lukas…'

'I love you, Rhiannon. Perhaps from the moment I saw you. Not at the reception, but the night before, on the beach. You were alone and I watched you. I felt like I knew you, like I'd finally met someone who might understand me.'

'You have,' Rhiannon said in an aching whisper, her voice raw with unshed tears.

Lukas walked slowly towards her, defenceless, open. Weak, vulnerable.

Strong.

'Will you forgive me? I've been a fool, a reluctant fool, and I'm so thankful you've stayed with me… You made me see myself.'

Rhiannon nodded, relief and joy rushing through her in a sweet, sweet wave as Lukas's arms came around her, drawing her close to him, drawing her home.

'You weren't really going to leave, were you? You scared the hell out of me, you know, with those bags.'

'I didn't want to leave,' Rhiannon admitted in a muffled voice, her head against his shoulder. 'But I was prepared to…I would have done anything to make you realise you loved me.'

'You were so sure?' Lukas teased, and Rhiannon gave a wavery laugh.

'No—and that was the worst part. Knowing it might all be for nothing…again.'

'But it isn't,' Lukas assured her, 'and it never will be.' He chuckled softly. 'Wait till my father hears this. He won't believe it.'

'He might,' Rhiannon replied with a smile. 'I think he is wiser than either of us.'

'We'll return to the island as soon as business is taken care of. If you don't mind…?'

She shook her head. 'And you don't mind that Annabel isn't a Petrakides?' Rhiannon knew in her heart that he didn't, but she still had to make sure.

'What I care about,' he told her, 'is that we're a family. And we are. Perhaps the first real one for both of us.'

Rhiannon nodded, and Lukas kissed a tear from her cheek. 'No more tears,' he whispered. 'For either of us.'

Only love…good, pure, wonderful.

Strong.

He's successful, powerful—and extremely sexy....
He also happens to be her boss! Used to getting his
own way, he'll demand what he wants from her—
in the boardroom and the bedroom....

Watch the sparks fly as these couples
work together—and play together!

IN BED WITH
THE BOSS

Don't miss any of the stories in April's collection!

MISTRESS IN PRIVATE
by JULIE COHEN

IN BED WITH HER ITALIAN BOSS
by KATE HARDY

MY TALL DARK GREEK BOSS
by ANNA CLEARY

HOUSEKEEPER TO
THE MILLIONAIRE
by LUCY MONROE

Available April 8
wherever books are sold.

www.eHarlequin.com

HPP0408NEW

HARLEQUIN *Presents*

Don't forget Harlequin Presents EXTRA
now brings you a powerful new collection
every month featuring four books!

Be sure not to miss any of the titles in

In the Greek Tycoon's Bed,

available May 13:

THE GREEK'S
FORBIDDEN BRIDE
by Cathy Williams

THE GREEK TYCOON'S
UNEXPECTED WIFE
by Annie West

THE GREEK TYCOON'S
VIRGIN MISTRESS
by Chantelle Shaw

THE GIANNAKIS BRIDE
by Catherine Spencer

www.eHarlequin.com   HPE0508

Be sure not to miss favorite
Harlequin Romance author

Lucy Gordon

in Harlequin Presents—
for one month only in May 2008!

THE ITALIAN'S PASSIONATE REVENGE

#2726

Elise Carlton is wary of being a trophy wife—except
to rich, well-dressed and devastatingly handsome
Vincente Farnese. It is no coincidence that this dark
Italian has sought her out for seduction....

Coming in June 2008 in Harlequin Romance:

The Italian's Cinderella Bride
by Lucy Gordon

www.eHarlequin.com   HP12726

HARLEQUIN *Presents*

Don't miss favorite author

Michelle Reid's

next book, coming in May 2008,
brought to you only
by Harlequin Presents!

THE MARKONOS BRIDE
#2723

Aristos is bittersweet for Louisa: here, she met
and married gorgeous Greek playboy Andreas
Markonos and produced a precious son. After
tragedy, Louisa was compelled to leave.
Five years later, she is back....

*Look out for more spectacular stories
from Michelle Reid, coming soon in 2008!*

www.eHarlequin.com   HP12723

REQUEST YOUR FREE BOOKS!

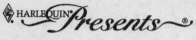 HARLEQUIN *Presents* ®

2 FREE NOVELS
PLUS 2
FREE GIFTS!

YES! Please send me 2 FREE Harlequin Presents® novels and my 2 FREE gifts (gifts are worth about $10). After receiving them, if I don't wish to receive any more books, I can return the shipping statement marked "cancel". If I don't cancel, I will receive 6 brand-new novels every month and be billed just $4.05 per book in the U.S. or $4.74 per book in Canada, plus 25¢ shipping and handling per book and applicable taxes, if any*. That's a savings of close to 15% off the cover price! I understand that accepting the 2 free books and gifts places me under no obligation to buy anything. I can always return a shipment and cancel at any time. Even if I never buy another book, the two free books and gifts are mine to keep forever.

106 HDN ERRW   306 HDN ERRL

Name _____ (PLEASE PRINT)

Address _____ Apt. # _____

City _____ State/Prov. _____ Zip/Postal Code _____

Signature (if under 18, a parent or guardian must sign)

Mail to the Harlequin Reader Service:
IN U.S.A.: P.O. Box 1867, Buffalo, NY 14240-1867
IN CANADA: P.O. Box 609, Fort Erie, Ontario L2A 5X3

Not valid to current subscribers of Harlequin Presents books.

Want to try two free books from another line?
Call 1-800-873-8635 or visit www.morefreebooks.com.

* Terms and prices subject to change without notice. N.Y. residents add applicable sales tax. Canadian residents will be charged applicable provincial taxes and GST. This offer is limited to one order per household. All orders subject to approval. Credit or debit balances in a customer's account(s) may be offset by any other outstanding balance owed by or to the customer. Please allow 4 to 6 weeks for delivery. Offer available while quantities last.

Your Privacy: Harlequin Books is committed to protecting your privacy. Our Privacy Policy is available online at www.eHarlequin.com or upon request from the Reader Service. From time to time we make our lists of customers available to reputable third parties who may have a product or service of interest to you. If you would prefer we not share your name and address, please check here. ☐

HP08